CONTENTS

THE LIFE & TIMES OF SARAH GOOD, ACCUSED WITCH

Salem Stories, Prequel

SANDRA WAGNER-WRIGHT

This is a work of fiction. Names, characters, organizations, places, and incidents are either a product of the author's imagination or are used fictitiously. Locales and public names are sometimes used for atmospheric purposes. Any resemblance to institutions or locales is completely coincidental.

Title/Sandra Wagner-Wright—first edition

ISBN: 978-1-7354132-5-9 (paperback)
ISBN: 978-1-7354132-7-3 (hardcover)
ISBN: 978-1-7354132-6-6 (eBook)

Cover: Execution of Ann Hibbins on Boston Common in 1656. From *Lynn & Surroundings* by Clarence W. Hobbes, 1886. Artist: Frank Thayer Merrill

CAST OF PRIMARY CHARACTERS IN ORDER OF APPEARANCE

- Sarah Solart Poole Good (1654–1692). Married Daniel Poole in 1682. Became a widow in 1683. Married William Good about 1685. Daughter Dorothy born about 1688. Daughter Mercy born about 1691 and died prior to Sarah's trial in June 1692. Executed for witchcraft July 19, 1692.

- Thomas Putnam, the Younger (Tom) (1651–1699). Sergeant in the Salem Village militia. Husband of Ann Carr Putnam. Father of Ann Putnam, the Younger. Eldest son of Lieutenant Thomas Putnam. Fought in the Great Swamp Battle. Brother-in-law to Reverend James Bayley. Supporter of Reverend Samuel Parris.

- Ann Carr Putnam (1661–1699). Married Thomas Putnam, the Younger in 1678. Mother of Ann Putnam, the Younger. Sister-in-law to Reverend James Bayley. Testified against Martha Corey and Rebecca Nurse during 1692 Witch Trials.

- Reverend James Bayley (1650–1707). Minister in Salem Village 1672–1680. Married to Mary Carr Bayley. Brother-in-law to Thomas Putnam, the Younger and Ann Carr Putnam.

- Mary Carr Bayley (1651–1688). Married to Reverend James Bayley. Sister of Ann Carr Putnam.

- Daniel Poole (ca. 1650 to ca. 1683). Married Sarah Solart in November 1682.

- William Good (ca. 1650 to early 1700s). Married Widow Sarah Solart Poole about 1686. Father of Dorothy Good and Mercy Good. After Sarah Good's execution in 1692, Good remarried in June 1693. Good looked after Dorothy Good until 1712 when he transferred her care to Deacon Benjamin Putnam. Over time, Dorothy lived in various households and gave birth to two children.

- Reverend Samuel Parris (1653–1720). Served as minister at Salem Village church 1688–1693. Father of Elizabeth (Betty) Parris. Uncle of Abigail Williams.

- Elizabeth (Betty) Parris (1680–1760). Daughter of Reverend Samuel Parris. One of the first children who appeared to suffer from witchcraft. She identified Sarah Good, Tituba, and Sarah Osborne as the source of her afflictions.

- Tituba (ca. 1662–?). Reverend Samuel Parris brought his slaves Tituba and her husband John Indian with him when he returned to Boston from Barbados. Tituba was the first person accused of witchcraft by Betty Parris and Abigail Williams. She was the first person to confess that she practiced witchcraft and had spoken to the devil. After the witch trials, Tituba remained at Boston Gaol because Samuel Parris refused to pay her prison fees. In April 1693, an unknown buyer purchased Tituba for the cost of her prison fees.

- Abigail Williams (1680–?). Niece of Reverend Samuel Parris. One of the first children who appeared to suffer from witchcraft. She identified Sarah Good, Tituba, and Sarah Osborne as source of her afflictions. Nothing is known of her fate after 1692.

- Dorothy Good (ca. 1687 to ca. 1721). Daughter of Sarah and William Good. Charged with witchcraft in March 1692. Remained in Boston Gaol until December 10, 1692.

- Mercy Good (ca. December 1691 to before June 1692). Daughter of Sarah and William Good.

- Ann Putnam, the Younger (1680–1716). Daughter of Ann Carr Putnam and Thomas Putnam, the Younger. One of the primary accusers during the 1692 Witch Trials.

- Elizabeth Hubbard (1674–?). Niece of Mistress Rachel Griggs, wife of Doctor William Griggs. She resided as a maidservant in the Griggs household. Accused Sarah Good and others of witchcraft.

- Magistrate John Hathorne (1641–1717). Merchant and magistrate of Salem Town. Related to Jonathan Corwin by marriage. Presided over witchcraft examinations at Salem Village and as a trial judge at the Court of Oyer and Terminer.

- Magistrate Jonathan Corwin (1640–1718). Merchant and magistrate of Salem Town. Related to John Hathorn by marriage. Presided over witchcraft examinations at Salem Village and as a trial judge at the Court of Oyer and Terminer.

- Sarah Osborne (ca. 1649–1692). At the time of her arrest, Osborne had been bedridden for some time and had not attended church for three years.

- Reverend Nicholas Noyes (1647–1717). Minister at Salem Town Church. Official chaplain of the Salem witch examinations and trials.

CHAPTER

Sarah Solart

January 1672
Solart House, Wenham, Massachusetts

I warm a clay tankard with hot water, swirling it around a few times before tossing the water into the fire. The flames hiss and crackle, sending sparks that nearly reach the ceiling. I grab a handful of sugar from across the table and throw it into the tankard, then add a splash of boiling water from the small kettle hanging over the fire.

"Careful ye don't burn yerself, girl."

I glance at the wingback chair near the fire, where Father slouches under blankets. His rheumy eyes, glittering beneath a velvet cap, focus on my hands.

"Ye've no need to worry, Father. This isn't the first toddy I've made for ye."

I muddle the ingredients, add a generous pour of rum, then more hot water, before mixing the concoction. Once I'm satisfied, I sprinkle nutmeg on the frothy surface. Father accepts the tankard, clasping his hands around the vessel's warm surface.

"Ye're a good daughter," he says before succumbing to a coughing fit.

I preen. I pick up my father's hand to rub my fingers against the calluses inside his palm. "All I ever want is to please ye."

Father sighs contentedly. "Ye've been the apple of my eye since the day ye were born." He brings a finger to his lips and winks. "Don't tell yer sisters."

I brush tears from my eyes with the back of my hands. Father isn't himself. His health fades more every day, and I am terrified of losing him. What if he leaves this world before I've wed? He provided for my older sisters on their wedding days, but Mother is of a less generous nature.

"Are ye cold, Father? Shall I get ye more blankets?" I ask, as though more blankets can disperse the sense of doom I feel.

"Nay. More blankets won't do me much good." He blows on his beverage and swallows. "I've sent Lewis Ford to find yer mother and young Abraham."

"Why?"

"Sarah." He gives me a pointed look. "Surely ye see my health isn't improving. If anything, it grows worse. I never know when I'm going to fall in a heap."

"Father—"

He puts his hand up. "I want to speak to ye before the others arrive. I want to explain—" *Wheeze. Rasp.* "I'm not well, child. One day, when I fall, I won't return to myself. I want to get my affairs in order, and I want ye to witness what I say so ye can tell yer brother John when his ship returns."

I feel as though I've been lanced through the chest with a spear. "Father," I say, wishing more than anything I had something to say. But I don't. The only thing that comes to mind is *John's ship isn't due to return for months.*

Father shrugs. "I may yet abide with everyone. I may not. Someone should know what is said. Someone who has no vested interest in the outcome. Someone of standing in the community. And that, my dear, is ye, my beloved daughter. Soon ye will marry and have a husband to look after yer affairs. Until then, stand yere ground."

The drawing room door opens to admit my mother and a gust of cold air. Her annoyance at being called away from her tasks is palpable. A few strands of her gray-streaked fair hair peek out from her coif, though she doesn't bother to push them off her face.

"Master Solart," she grumbles, "the boy told me ye wish to see me. I'm very busy at the moment, so it would be considerate of ye if we could defer whatever conversation ye wish to have."

"I fear the conversation must take place now while I have full command of my faculties. I shall set matters in writing later, but I want to present my will to ye verbally. I want our daughter to bear witness to my remarks, and also young Lewis and Abraham."

Mother raises her eyebrows. "Ye want *indentured servants* to witness our business affairs?"

"Of course. They have no vested interest in the outcome, so their testimony will be compelling if matters go to the quarterly court."

Father drops his empty tankard and starts coughing.

I jump up and assist him into an upright sitting position, but he waves me off and says, "Don't fuss, girl." He breathes slowly for several minutes. Mother and I wait. "Ye see," he goes on, "it is as I said. There is no way to know how long I shall be among ye."

The double doors open again, admitting our two servants. They shuffle into the room with lowered gazes. Lewis Ford has been with us two years and has another five on his indenture. Abraham Martin joined us last harvest time. He's a timid soul and does his duties without speaking.

"Ye summoned us, sir?" Lewis asks.

"I did, and now that we are assembled, we can begin. I admonish both of ye to pay special attention to my verbal will, which I am about to impart. Ye may be called upon to testify about what ye hear today."

"Yes, sir," Lewis says. "Rest assured, we will not fail ye."

"Shouldn't we wait until John returns?" Mother asks. "He is yere eldest son."

"Who knows when that will be, or if his ship will return at all," Father replies bluntly. "I am adamant. I shall present my verbal will now. Lewis, Abraham—ye will both remember it and testify to the same. As will ye, my loyal wife. And if yer memories dim, Sarah will remind ye. Shall we begin?"

The four of us nod silently.

Father clears his throat. "I, John Solart of Wenham, being of sound mind, do make this, my verbal will, before witnesses. I am often troubled with fainting fits and apprehend I may not have long to live. After my death, my wife, Elizabeth Solart, shall have the use of my whole estate for herself during the time of her widowhood, and also for the bringing up of our children."

Father stops speaking and coughs for several minutes. When I rise to assist him, he waves me away again and continues.

"If my wife should remarry, then I give her one-third of my estate, and the rest shall be divided among my children." He smiles. "There, that was not so difficult after all. Sarah, there's a good girl. Make me another toddy. The rest of ye," he adds, looking specifically at Mother, "may go about yer *important* duties."

"We won't fail ye, sir," Lewis says and motions Abraham to follow him out of the room.

I begin rinsing out the tankard.

"Master Solart." Mother's voice has a slight tremor. Glancing over my shoulder, I observe her peering at Father with tears in her eyes. "I'm overcome with yere generosity."

"Why? It is only yere just due," Father says without looking at her directly. "And if ye are to raise our children, ye will need every penny. Now, dry yere eyes and be about yere business."

He flicks his fingers toward the door, and Mother departs. I work on his toddy for a few minutes, the only noise disrupting the silence that of the crackling fire in the hearth. Finally, I put nutmeg on the frothy surface again and say, "I have yer toddy, Father."

"Thank ye. Shall ye stay with me a little while until the fire dies down a bit? I should hate to expire alone."

C H A P T E R

Sarah Solart

September 1672
Solart House

My brother John smells like the sea and fresh air, the opposite of the dusty gloom in my father's house. Or, more accurately, my mother's now.

John grabs my right hand. "We can do this," John says.

I shrug and pull my hand away. *What else is there to do?*

"Ye don't understand. Ye were away when Father died." I clench my fists. "The inquest was wrong. He never took his own life! He wouldn't do such a sinful thing."

John shakes his head and motions for me to sit on the bench next to the door. He sits down next to me and takes both my hands into his.

"Sarah, ye must accept the truth. This past April, Father walked into the lake and didn't walk out again; I don't blame him. From what ye tell me, his fits were getting worse. Father always faced matters head-on. So he set his affairs in order and left us. Truth be told, I think he waited as long as he did so he could speak to me and put matters in writing. Once he did that . . ." He pauses, spreading his hands in a way that says, *What else did he have left to live for?*

I hold my tongue. I knew Father better than John ever did, but I'll never persuade him from his opinion.

"Today is a formality." John squeezes my hands. "We attend court, the magistrates divide our property, and we all move forward."

"Ye mean, ye'll go back to sea."

John smiles, his eyes crinkling. "I can probably do two more runs to the West Indies before we lay over for winter. If ye weren't a girl, I'd get ye a billet. There's nothing like it. At sea, I feel free. Ashore, I'm pulled apart by expectations. Besides, I don't want to farm. Nothing could suit me less."

I try to give him a smile but fail. "Ye could run the ordinary."

"I could, but I won't."

Before I can answer, Mother comes into the room with her *friend*. Shortly after the initial inventory of my father's estate became public, Ezekiel Woodward began consoling my mother on her grievous loss. My father left an estate worth five hundred pounds, a successful business, and several children too young to receive their fair share of his bequests. Mother isn't interested in any of it, except as a source of income, but I suspect Master Woodward is.

"Are ye ready?" Mother asks. "The magistrates won't appreciate it if we're late to court."

Master Woodward touches Mother's arm. "Mistress Solart, we need to depart. The servants began walking an hour ago."

"Yes, thank ye, Master Woodward. Come along, children," Mother says, as if I am not nineteen years old and my brother twenty-two. Mother adjusts her hat and sweeps through the door. I roll my eyes and follow. I think John chuckles behind me, but I'm not sure. He'll sail away and leave me here to serve in our tavern and look after my siblings until it's too late for me to marry. It's so unfair.

I almost enjoy the walk to Ipswich. It's a dry day and some of the leaves are turning, though the weather remains warm. Mother walks with Master Woodward as if she's on a stroll, and I wonder what he expects to gain.

Father gave her everything while she remains a widow, but *not* if she remarries. Why would she even consider such a thing? But watching her gesture at leaves swirling in the wind and incline her head coquettishly toward Master Woodward, I suspect she won't remain a grieving widow much longer.

After briskly walking for a couple of hours, we reach Meetinghouse Green in the center of Ipswich and make our way to Spark's Ordinary, where the quarterly court meets. Standing close to the meetinghouse, the tavern is easy to spot. People gather outside, watching new arrivals enter the clapboard building. Mother lifts her head as if the people outside are beneath her, and perhaps they are.

Inside, I spot our family servants seated at the back of the room. Master Woodward guides Mother forward to the first row of seats. John and I follow behind. The room fills with people who have business with the court.

Three magistrates preside over court business, mostly property and inheritances. Eventually, the bailiff calls our servants forward to testify about Father's verbal will. Mother glares at them as they come forward to stand before the bar.

Lewis is visibly nervous and shuffles from foot to foot.

"State yer name," Magistrate Hathorne says.

"Lewis Ford, Yer Worship."

"Ye say ye were in the room when John Solart declared his verbal will?"

"Yes, Master." Lewis bobs his head. "Abraham Martin and myself. And Mistress Solart. And young Mistress Solart."

"And what did John Solart declare?"

"He said . . . he said he was ill with fainting fits and didn't think he had long to live. He said Widow Solart could use his entire estate unless she remarried. Then she would only have a third portion, with the rest going to his children."

"Ye are certain of this?"

Lewis nods vigorously. "I've repeated it to myself every day lest I forget."

"And ye." Master Hathorne turns his attention to Abraham Martin. "Do ye concur with this testimony?"

"Aye," he confirms with a stalwart nod.

"And ye depose the same as Lewis Ford?"

"Aye."

"Very well. Ye may return to yer seats." Master Hathorne turns to the other judges. "Do ye have concerns in this matter?"

An older gentleman clears his throat. "I do," he rasps. "I call Widow Solart to the bar."

Mother gasps and clutches her right hand to her heart. I feel a sense of alarm. Will Mother be interrogated? And, if she is, will she testify to the truth of Father's will or try to twist it so she won't have her share reduced if she remarries?

Master Woodward escorts Mother from her seat to the bar and stands behind her for a moment before returning to his seat.

"Widow Solart, I am Master Symonds, a merchant in this town. I wish to learn more about this verbal will yer husband made. What can ye tell the court?"

"My husband granted me his estate so I could raise his children," Mother says rather stiltedly.

"The previous witnesses noted yer eldest son, also called John, was not present. Where was he?"

Mother pats her chest again. "He was at sea, of course. But my husband already gave him a parcel of land, in writing, which was to be his portion." Mother nods her chin for emphasis, as though this should settle the matter. When nobody responds, she wrings her hands. "But then," she adds, "John came home between the time my husband declared his will and his decease. It was then that my son vowed that he did not require the land since he would follow the sea."

"Anything further?" Master Symonds asks.

"Only that he said again I was to have use of the estate so long as I was a widow, and if I married again, I should have one-third of the estate for myself," she says. I find it hard to conceal my look of shock. Mother is telling the full truth. "Son John would have a double portion from the remainder, and everything else would be divided among his younger brother and sisters."

"Thank ye. It being the time of nooning, we shall retire and rule on this matter when court resumes."

Sarah Solart

Spark's Ordinary, Ipswich

Mother, Master Woodward, John, and I convene at a small table at the back of the ordinary. Mother purchases ale and bowls of stew for everyone. I'm not sure when the stew was prepared, but there are globs of fat on the surface. I soak them into my bread.

"Why didn't the magistrates call on John?" Mother asks. "Why did I have to testify?"

"I wasn't present for Father's verbal will, Mother," John mutters. "And ye're executor of Father's estate. They only called the servants for corroboration."

"They didn't call Sarah. She was there."

"But not on the record as a witness," John replies. "Have ye finished, Sarah? Let's get some air."

John offers me his hand and nods to Mother. I accept, following him out of the overcrowded tavern alongside a slew of others. The air feels crisp on my cheeks.

"What do ye think they'll decide?" I ask.

John shrugs. "They'll probably go along with what Father devised. Ye'll help Mother with the tavern until ye marry. No surprise there. I'll be at sea. Our two older sisters have their own families to look after. It will all seem normal soon."

I swallow hard. "But Father is gone forever."

"That he is."

A drum sounds behind us.

"Court begins," John says, sighing. "Let's hope we finish our business first and can go back to Wenham."

By the time John and I filter into the courthouse again, Mother and Master Woodward are already seated, with their heads as close together as is decent in public. They whisper something that I can't make out.

Master Hathorne calls the court to order.

"In the matter of John Solart's estate, the court grants administration of the estate to Elizabeth Solart, the widow. An inventory presents a clear estate valued at five hundred pounds, out of which we order the widow to receive one hundred sixty-five pounds."

Mother hisses under her breath. No doubt she expected the *entire* estate.

"John, the eldest son, will receive a double portion of eighty-four pounds out of the homestead, on condition he wait until his mother's death to receive it."

Beside me, John sucks in a breath.

"If she doesn't spend it all," he mutters to me.

The magistrate drones on, oblivious to our responses. He picks up a second parchment. "Two daughters received their portion when they married. Six children remain. They will each receive forty-two pounds as they come of age."

Forty-two pounds! That means . . . I hardly dare hope . . . I keep my fingers in my lap and count them. In two years, I'll be rich. Every man in the colony will want me for his wife.

For the first time since Father died, I feel hopeful.

Thomas Putnam, the Younger

October 1672
Ingersoll's Ordinary, Salem Village

Father and I enter Ingersoll's Ordinary, leaving our swords by the door. Strangers going to and from Boston glance up from their food, noting our entry, before turning their attention back to their own affairs.

"This way." Father leads us to a table in the great room's back corner.

Deacon Ingersoll, the robust innkeeper, comes to the table with two tankards of ale. He gives me a swift nod but addresses my father. "Ye brought yer boy, then," he says. I inwardly grimace. *Do I really look so young?*

Father lays his hand on my arm, as though sensing my discomfort.

"He's nineteen now," he replies. "Time he learns how things are done. He'll be an important part of this town once he's a householder."

"Aye," Ingersoll agrees. For a moment, he openly studies me, and I make sure to hold my chin high and keep my posture straight. I don't look away from his stare. "Ye do right to bring him along," he concedes at last. "Will the committee be joining us?"

"I sent word for them to meet here. I have a reply from the General Court."

"Go to the small room. No reason for the village to hear our business."

We grab our ale and head to the back room. There's a small fire in the grate, though the weather hasn't fully turned yet. But ye never know. Village leaders trickle into the room. We sit around a long table, my father in the one armchair at its head. He lifts his tankard, taking a generous sip of its contents.

"Will we have our own church or not?" Master Wilkins growls, initiating the meeting.

"The short answer is Jehovah heard our prayer and grants us a way forward," Father replies.

Thomas Flint strokes his chin. "A sure sign of his mercy," he says, "for if we remain much longer without the privileges of religion, we'll become worse than the native people surrounding us. We have waited long enough. Too many of us cannot or will not walk to Salem Town for meetings."

The conversation devolves into the usual bickering and complaints about the church in Salem Town leaving our village to its own devices, of which we presently have none.

Father raises his hands to get the men's attention. "The General Court approved having a church in Salem Village built," he notes. "We can have a congregation with our own minister. However—"

Village leaders interrupt by standing with broad smiles, clasping their hands and shouting blessings and praise to Jehovah. When the prayers of thanksgiving subside and we all resume our seats, my father continues. "Jehovah graciously blesses us, but tasks remain. We can form our own church and call a minister to mind our flock, but we cannot form a fully independent church until the minister is ordained, and the church in Salem Town must give its approval first."

Deacon Ingersoll calls a servant to pour out more ale. The village leaders become silent for several minutes, drinking and thinking.

Joseph Hutchinson stands to speak. "I suggest we build our meetinghouse immediately. It must be here, at the center of our village and close to this ordinary, so worshippers can receive refreshments as needed."

"Aye," everyone agrees.

"Therefore," Master Hutchinson continues, "I shall donate an acre of land from my meadow for the meetinghouse and suggest that since Master Flint is a carpenter, he shall oversee the design and construction of the new building."

"I think we can all agree to yer suggestions, and everyone will greatly appreciate yer donation of land at the heart of our village," my father says. "Master Flint, how long will it take to construct an adequate meetinghouse?"

Thomas Flint reaches into his pocket to retrieve a small slip of parchment, which he passes down the table. "As it happens, I've given some thought to the structure. It won't be as comfortable as this ordinary, but 'twill serve the purpose."

Flint proceeds to describe a boxlike structure similar to a house with an entry porch and two latticed windows with small diamond-shaped panes on each side.

"And inside?" Deacon Ingersoll asks.

"I should think plain, in the first instance. People can sit on benches facing the pulpit area, so the minister can be heard without distractions. No offense, Deacon Ingersoll, but people's eyes do wander while Master Bayley preaches."

"Aye."

"Walls?" my father asks.

"We'll use pine for the clapboards and whitewash it on the inside. The beams and such will be oak. If there are no questions or suggestions, I'll get things started and assign each household items to produce. We should be able to raise the church by next summer."

My father nods. "All in favor of Master Flint's plans, say aye."

Everyone echoes their agreement. My father knocks his knuckles on the table.

"There is only the matter of a minister left to discuss," my father adds, "and that is the most important matter of all."

"Are ye aware of anyone qualified for the office of minister and willing to serve our community on an annual basis?" Deacon Ingersoll asks. "We must, after all, be sure the candidate is of sound preparation and compatible with our beliefs and concerns."

"And most of all, that he pleases Jehovah," Master Flint adds. "Do ye know of anyone, Deacon Putnam?"

My father strokes his chin. "James Bayley, the young man who preached to us this past year, is the best choice. He knows us; we know him. He graduated from Harvard, and he's a full member of the church at Newbury, so we need have no concerns regarding his status among the Elect who are destined for heaven. And . . ." My father pauses. "Master Bayley returns shortly with his new bride, a Mistress Mary Carr from Salisbury, which means he will establish his family among us here." He spreads his hands. "See how Jehovah provides for us."

"Aye," Deacon Ingersoll agrees. "Everyone who wishes to hire Master Bayley as our minister for the next year, say aye."

Once again, the decision is unanimous. Deacon Ingersoll calls for more ale.

Ann Carr

One Week Later
Entering Salem Village

The wind comes up, swirling colorful autumn leaves around our wagon. Master Bayley holds the reins, my sister sitting next to him; I sit on the side. Salem Village is not appealing. People stop to gaze at us as we drive past them. The farmers wear swords at their belts, as if expecting an attack at any moment. They call to my brother-in-law, who stops the wagon to greet them and introduce my sister Mary as his new wife. The men dip their hats, and the women curtsy. My sister says she hopes to see them at the meetinghouse this week so she can know them better. Sometimes she introduces me; other times she forgets. Mary is excited, nervous, and attached to her new husband. She pats his arm constantly, as if he will disappear. I feel an uneasy premonition of doom but have no reason for it.

I hadn't wanted to move away from Salisbury, but my sister raised me, and I simply couldn't refuse her pleas to move with her so she wouldn't be friendless in a new place.

Master Bayley stops the wagon in front of Lieutenant Thomas Putnam's large house, jumps to the ground, and helps my sister down while I scramble off the conveyance. A servant comes out to lead the horse and wagon away. Master Bayley wraps an arm around my sister and helps her into the house, leaving me to trail behind.

"I need to speak to Master Putnam," he says to me, already striding down the narrow hallway, easing out of sight. "Take care of my wife."

As though I've got a say in the matter.

I swallow hard, turning to behold my sister. A breath later, a serving maid emerges at my side and hands me two small tankards of beer and drapes a damp clout over my arm. "Master Bayley asked me to bring ye refreshments and a clout for his wife. I hope she isn't unwell."

"Just tired from the long journey," I reply, though I truthfully worry she might have a fever.

"We're preparing rooms for yer party. Master and Mistress Bayley will be on the second floor, and ye'll have a room in the garret. It isn't large, but better than sleeping near a married couple."

The maid winks and turns away. Mary takes the cloth from my arm and wipes her face before drinking her beer. She pats my hand. "It was only a bit of dizziness, my dear," she reassures me, though the flush to her cheeks says otherwise. "I'm better now."

Master Bayley approaches with several people. "May I introduce my wife, Mistress Mary Bayley, and her sister, Mistress Ann Carr."

We stand and curtsy. Mary produces a dazzling smile that lights her eyes, but I can only muster an uninspired nod. I've no desire to impress anyone.

"I am Deacon Putnam," the tall, older man says. "Welcome to our home. We thought ye would like to rest here for one or two days while yer own home is prepared. Master Bayley has been staying there already, I'm aware, but my wife"—he pauses, eyes sparkling as he looks down at the middle-aged woman beside him—"tells me it lacks a *woman's touch.*"

"Well, Mr. Putnam, it most certainly does," she replies, swatting playfully at his arm.

He takes her arm and says, "Allow me to introduce my wife, Mistress Mary Putnam."

"We'll be a family of *Marys*, then," my sister jokes as she curtsies again.

"I'm sure we'll be fast friends," the woman replies, stepping back.

"And this strapping young man," Lieutenant Putnam continues, "is my heir, Thomas."

A slender youth steps forward. He bows to my sister and then to me. I curtsy in return. His gaze lingers on my face for a few moments before he winks at me and steps back. I gasp with surprise at his audacity and watch him from the corner of my lowered eyes. I don't know whether to be flattered or insulted.

Ann Carr

August 1673
Salem Village Parsonage

My niece is unbearably small, her face a pale mask peeking out from the winding sheet.

Less than a month old and already she faces Jehovah's terrible justice. My sister, still suffering from childbirth, sits by her infant's small wooden box with tears streaming down her cheeks. She will not be comforted. Master Bayley is equally distraught but doesn't show it.

"God will send us other children," he tells Mary.

"I don't *want* other children. I want my baby!" Mary sniffles while Master Bayley turns away.

I put my arm around her shaking shoulders and whisper, "I've heard it said that Jesus gathers innocent lambs to himself, so that heaven may be replenished."

Even as I say the words, I don't believe them. Neither does my sister. She buries her head in my shoulder and sobs, and I stroke her hair, searching for something to say.

"Ye must trust Jehovah's judgment," I settle on. "If ye question him, he may not let ye have more children, and how can ye refuse the little souls waiting to be born?"

My sister hiccups and her tears slow for a moment.

"I don't know why God punishes me so."

Reverend Bayley walks over to us. "I'm sorry, Mistress Bayley, but it is time. The Putnams are here to walk with us."

"I'll get my hat," she says.

"No," he says gently. "Ye are not strong enough to walk the distance. Ye need to recover yere strength and resume yere duties. The loss of Baby Mary is a great tribulation, a great test of our trust in Jehovah. But her soul has little sin to weigh it down. Jehovah's early call to her is a blessing. Truly. Ye must accept that."

He draws my sister away. Deacon Putnam and his son place the lid on my niece's coffin and take it outside, where they load it onto a handcart. Tom says he will push it, and I smile in gratitude before I bow my head. My sister stays inside the house. I hope now that my niece is no longer present, Mary can begin to heal.

The drummer goes before us to announce our solemn passage as we walk through the village. The people we pass stand respectfully, bowing their heads. I scuff my boots on the path in frustration at Jehovah's decision to take back my niece but keep my thoughts to myself.

It takes almost three hours to walk to the barren land everyone calls Ye Burying Point. It sits just outside the town, as though the occupants' souls have been banished from the living. The handcart is awkward on the rutted road, bouncing my niece's small coffin on the cart bed. Sweat trickles down my face and back as the day warms.

At the burying point, a cooling wind blows in from the sea. Tom pushes the handcart until we reach a gravesite with soil mounded around it. The grave itself is heartbreakingly tiny. I hear Reverend Bayley sigh and wonder if he will allow himself to show emotion. He was sitting next to my sister, holding her hand when Baby Mary made a slight whooshing sound and took her last breath—but his expression had never changed, even as he'd prayed for the repose of her soul.

Deacon Putnam and his son lift my niece's coffin and carefully lower it into the open grave. Reverend Bayley raises his hands and prays, but the wind whips his words away. Then, he lifts a shovelful of dirt and tosses the soil into the grave. It almost covers the coffin. I pick up small rocks and throw them inside. They clatter against the box. After everyone throws in a handful of dirt or rocks, Deacon Putnam and his son begin burying the coffin. Within an hour, there is only a fresh mound of rocks and soil to mark the place.

Deacon Putnam and my brother-in-law swiftly walk away.

Tom grabs the handcart handles. "They're going to stop at the church for a bit to meet with the minister and deacons. Would ye care to accompany me back to the village?"

I give him a quiet nod, and we fall into an easy stride. Now that it's over, I feel spent and empty.

"Ye can sit in the cart if ye're tired," he offers, clearly picking up on my mood. "I know it's been a long day for ye."

"Thank ye, but I can walk. Why did ye come to the grave?"

"To offer support, I suppose. I knew Father wouldn't push the cart, and Reverend Bayley is beyond exhausted."

"And me?" I ask. "Did ye think me too weak?"

Tom shrugs. "No, but the cart is heavier than it looks, and grief is a great burden. I'm sure it's been a difficult two months at yer house."

"It's been . . ." My voice catches in my throat. How *has* it been? Miserable doesn't even begin to cover it. I recall flashes of Baby Mary's blue lips. The soft and dire sound my niece made right before taking her last breath. Sobs pour out of me.

Tom puts down the cart and places his hand on my shoulder. I hiccup and swipe my face with the back of my hand.

"There, lass. 'Twill be all right. Ye take care of everyone, but no one takes care of ye. Let it out and ye'll feel better."

I fist my hands. "It's just so unfair," I say, my vision blurred by tears. "Three months ago, we were all anticipating a new baby—a new beginning. Now, *this*."

"Careful, Mistress Carr. No matter what ye feel, ye canna be sayin' that. Yer brother-in-law's the minister, after all." He gives me a look that's almost like a warning. "Jehovah doesn't make mistakes. Yer sister will recover and have other children. Of that, I am sure."

Of that, I am sure also. That is what is expected of her, of course.

Tom picks up the cart handles again. "Come. I want to stop for a meal before we get home."

We walk in silence, eventually arriving at a small ordinary near the roadway. Tom orders ale and venison ragout for both of us before guiding me to a table at the back. He helps me to my seat and gives me a look that seems bold but probably isn't. It's just that my thoughts turn to Tom more than they should. He's so sure of himself. Maybe that's because his father is such an important man in the village. But I think it's more than that.

"How old are ye now?" Tom asks.

I jump at the sound of his voice.

"What? What did ye say?" I stammer.

"I asked how old ye are."

I don't know what to say. I'm twelve, and he's, well, much older. Too old for me to be thinking about. Just as I open my mouth to deflect Tom's question, the barmaid arrives with our food. I inhale the rich aroma wafting from the ragout.

"The food smells wonderful." I dip my spoon into the bowl.

Tom sighs and nods his head. "Eat up," he says. "Ye're too thin."

The ragout is flavorful, and we eat in companionable silence. For the first time since my sister gave birth, I scrape my spoon on the bottom of a bowl and smile.

When we go outside, Tom picks up the handcart again, and we resume our return journey.

C H A P T E R

Ann Carr

August 1673
Salem Village Parsonage

My eyes pop open when light filters through the small diamond window-panes in my chamber. *Dawn at last.* For the first time since my niece died, I'm filled with happy anticipation. Everyone in Salem Village and most of Salem Town will be at the church raising—and most importantly, Tom will be there. Two months ago, he went out with other young men to fell oak trees for the rafters. Now, the logs lie like fallen soldiers in Hutchinson's field where the church will begin to rise later today.

Whenever I could steal away from my grieving sister's side, I walked to the building site to watch Tom and the other young men trim the branches and shape the timber into pleasing patterns for the church rafters. At first, they worked with axes to remove extra branches. Then they started using chisels. Every day, as long as there was light, Tom carved the logs with delicate grooves and designs; he'd work for hours, with immense concentration. Sometimes, he'd see me and wave before returning to his task.

After making myself decent, I arrive downstairs to see my brother-in-law pulling on his boots.

"Good, ye're here," he says. "Help yer sister eat. I must pray a blessing on today's work."

Reverend Bayley puts on his hat and leaves.

I shrug and turn to my sister. "So, Mary, it's a great day for yer husband. Get changed so we can help with the food."

Mary looks up from her full porridge bowl and moves her spoon around. I can already tell what her answer will be. "Ye go. Everyone will either avoid looking at me or ask if I'm well when they can see quite clearly that I am not."

"Shall I stay with ye?"

"Don't be silly," she insists. I should be ashamed for feeling a sense of relief. "Ye need to mix with the other girls and keep yer eye out for young Tom Putnam."

My cheeks warm with embarrassment. "I don't know what ye mean."

A smile ghosts across Mary's lips. "I've seen ye watch him. Ye'll be able to see him better outside. And, if ye go, it won't be as obvious I'm not there. Please."

Shouts and the sound of mallets banging wood into place filter in from outside.

I shift my feet. "If ye're certain?"

"I am. Leave me with my grief, and tell me everything when ye return."

At the building site, more people than I've ever seen in one place swarm the area. Men work on the rafters, though they probably won't be placed today. Other men prepare the four sides of the building so they can be raised on the morrow. Different teams of men work at each of the structure's four corners, placing vertical posts into the sills connected to the stone floor. Master Flint walks around the site inspecting everyone's progress, muttering that everything must be straight.

I look around for Tom and see him holding a post upright against his shoulder while others make the attachment. He grunts with exertion, his shirt stretching across his shoulders. Sweat pours down his face. When the post is straight, Tom uses a mallet to pound round wooden pegs through perfectly matched holes.

Once the posts are secure, men climb up to begin setting the rafters, and above them, the framework for the roof. I watch the scene until the bright sunlight makes me dizzy.

This, I think, *must be how things looked when Noah built the ark.*

When the sun reaches its highest point, men on the ground begin shouting it's time for the nooning. Mistress Ingersoll and other women set up a table with wooden trenchers. By the outside fire, cooking pots bubble with venison stew. The men fill their trenchers first, followed by women and children. I put beakers of small beer on a tray and distribute them to people resting on the ground. Children chase each other near the building site. Soon, the men go back to work, and by sunset, the walls on the ground are ready to be raised.

Tom Putnam, the Younger

The Next Day

The view from the church rafters takes my breath away. I've been on house roofs before, but this is the highest I've ever been. I can see all the way to Salem Town and the glistening harbor in the distance beyond it. I feel like flying and shake my head to recover myself.

"Keep a good grip on the rafter," the man next to me says, and I nod. "If ye like endless sky, ye should sail with me. I'll put ye in the crow's nest. Nothing but sea, sky, arcing dolphins, and flying fish. Not at the same time, a'course."

I take up the slack in his rope. "Ye from Salem?"

"Aye. I'd shake yer hand, but we need to keep our grips," he says with a grin.

"Ye work on ships. Why mingle with us?" I inquire.

"I've spent time with a spyglass in the crow's nest, but I've never balanced on roof rafters, preparing to pull up a wall. I came for a lark." The man winks.

"Mind ye don't slip," I advise and glance at the others on the roof. "Pull yer ropes!"

The edge of the wall lifts.

Men on the ground hook long pikes against the wall's side and push it upward while my crew and I pull the ropes, hand over hand.

"Heave! Heave! Heave!" the call goes out.

"Keep 'er straight!" Flint shouts.

Slowly the wall straightens and continues its journey to the rafters.

My shoulder muscles burn. Sweat pours down my face and into my eyes.

Finally, the wall stands square. The men on top secure it to the rafters and begin moving to the next side of the building, where rafters await the wall laying on the ground.

"When do we get a break?" the sailor asks.

"Nooning," I grunt.

Ann Carr

I bring a tray filled with sausages to the serving table. The line of tired men seems never-ending, but Tom has yet to appear.

"Ann," I hear somebody say from behind me.

"Oh, Reverend Bayley, I didn't realize ye were here."

My brother-in-law gives me a disapproving look. "That's because yer eyes were on the roof and not the wall. I worked with the pikemen."

Of course ye did. Ye don't have the courage to balance on the rafters.

"Do ye need anything else?" I ask rather dryly.

"I'll take ale when ye bring it around. Don't dawdle."

"Yes, Reverend Bayley."

"Ann," a feminine voice calls.

"Yes, Mistress Ingersoll?"

"I'll take yer place here. Ye and the other girls take ale for the workers and bring back their trenchers. They need washing."

At the bar inside, I grab several tankards and begin walking over the grassy meadow, trying to spot Tom. I see him leaning against a fence post at the side of the meadow, dipping his fingers into his trencher. I hold on to the last of my tankards until I can walk over to the fence.

"Ye look like ye can use something to drink," I say with a smile, holding out the ale.

Tom glances up and grins. "I can. Sit by me while I finish my meal." He pats the ground.

I hand him his ale and cross my ankles to sit gracefully, but I lose my balance and plop down on my bottom with my skirts billowing around me. I'm *mortified*. Tom coughs and draws on his ale, smothering a laugh.

"Mistress Carr, are ye quite alright?"

"O' course. Just a bit off balance," I insist. "I could never work on the rafters like ye do; I'm much too clumsy."

Tom clears his throat. "It's not a job for a young woman such as yerself. Ye have to be strong to work the ropes."

"Ye certainly are that." My cheeks heat, and I look away.

"Thank ye, Mistress Carr. I merely do what is needed." For a moment, we're quiet. When he speaks again, his voice is softer, kinder. "Has yer sister recovered from her loss, now that yer niece is . . . ?"

I shake my head before he can continue further and pick at the sparse grass. "I doubt she ever will. But I pray her grief may lessen. Otherwise, I fear for her health."

"And what does Reverend Bayley say?"

"That she must trust Jehovah."

Tom shrugs. "There's not much else she can do."

We sit quietly together until the drum sounds. Tom stands, brushes himself off, and reaches out his hand. I accept it and allow him to pull me into a standing position—which he does gracefully, as if I'm made of air. He then passes me his tankard and trencher.

"Time to raise the last two walls and secure the roof." He puts his hands in his pockets. "We can walk together to the building site, if ye like."

I'd like that very much.

"Since we're going the same way, it seems a logical choice," I reply.

"Indeed."

I try to think of something clever to say, but my mind is blank.

"Please be careful," I say when we reach the roof's access point. "It's a long way to fall."

"Rest assured, I've no plans to slip."

I shade my eyes with my hand and watch Tom climb to his perch.

Master Flint stops by my side. "Are ye well, Mistress? Ye need to move. We have workers coming through here."

"Aye, I'm fine, Master Flint. Just lost my way for a moment."

I mutter a quick prayer for Tom's safety and return to the ordinary.

Ann Carr

September 1673
Salem Village Parsonage

I grab my hat, pull it over the coif that covers my hair, and call to the maid behind me. "Hurry up, Dorcas, ye can't be late for the meeting."

"Aye, Mistress."

I hold my skirts up and trot by my sister, who marches across the space between the parsonage and the new church.

Bang-bang-bang!

I jump at the sound of drumming nearby.

"Hurry up! The drummer is almost at the church," Mary mutters. "Ye know I don't like walking into a meeting by myself."

"Then ye shouldn't have left first."

The drummer strides around us and reaches the door before we do. Inside, he unfastens the drum straps and leaves the instrument in the back corner. Farmers hanging up their swords and knives on hooks by the door nod to us.

We walk through the whispering crowd to the space reserved for us at the front of the women's side. The whispers become quiet, but just as I settle into my seat, the Putnam family enters. The women take their seats behind me while the men sit across the aisle.

I glance up to see Tom watching me. He winks before sitting on the rough bench and stretching his legs out in front of him. I turn my attention to my brother-in-law, who keeps his face bland while shaking hands with those who come forward to greet him.

Does he get nervous before preaching? I wonder to myself, my eyes still locked on the neutral and even empty expression on his face as he makes his way around the room, greeting people. *Probably not, but he's a careful man.*

At home, I often watch Reverend Bayley practice his sermons. First, he makes notes on small pieces of parchment that fit in the palm of his hand, so he can keep track of his ideas. Then, he paces back and forth in the parlor, muttering to himself and glancing at his hand. After two or three days, he's memorized most of his message.

Deacon Putnam takes his place at a table just below the pulpit. A large hourglass sits on the table. Once the sermon starts, he will turn the hourglass over three times before the morning session ends, and parishioners can re-fresh themselves before the afternoon meeting.

I wish we could go back to the house, but no one is allowed to leave. Mary says it's a good opportunity for us to meet with our neighbors and find out how we can serve them. She says we have to set an example for the women, but I don't see why. Everyone knows their job is to support their husbands, run their households, and produce children. When I tell Mary this, she says we can encourage them to be content.

I compose myself and watch my brother-in-law climb into the pulpit. He stands in silence for several minutes until the entire space becomes still. Everyone keeps their eyes forward. Reverend Bayley lifts his hands for the congregation to stand in prayer. I close my eyes and try to look devout. His prayer goes on for so long I think I shall faint before it finishes. He thanks Jehovah for saving Israel, for sending faithful preachers, and for sending him to Salem Village. Finally, he stops speaking and steps back so Deacon Ingersoll can lead the congregation in Psalm 1. The deacon sings each line in meter so people can repeat it after him, ending with "But the way of the ungodly shall perish." When the endless psalm is over, I resume my seat with a flounce that earns me Mary's disapproving eye.

Finally, we can sit in peace with our own thoughts.

Just as my mind begins to drift, Reverend Bayley looks directly at the con-gregation and recites from the prophet Amos in a voice so dramatic, it makes me shiver. "Woe to them that are at ease in Zion, and trust in the mountain of Samaria, which are named chief of the nations, to whom the house of Israel came!" he says in a sonorous voice. Those in attendance sit rigidly, rapt by every word he speaks. "Ye that put far away the evil day and cause the seat of violence to come near."

My brother-in-law looks over the benches for several minutes and then begins his sermon, arguing that a sinful sense of security is the disease of last times, that his listeners err because they banish any thought of a day of trouble.

I squirm with acute boredom. *On and on and on he speaks.* Every time I think he may stop, he glances at his palm and admonishes us again. Deacon Putnam turns the hourglass once, twice, thrice. My stomach growls. I even catch Mary dozing in an upright position. Finally, Reverend Bayley pronounces a closing prayer and dismisses the congregation for nooning.

People stand with creaking joints and estimate how long they must wait to use the necessary. Some people brought food with them, but we purchase small beer and stew with fresh bread at the ordinary. Too soon, the drum beats again. Everyone returns to their assigned places, and Reverend Bayley launches into another sermon.

When the day is over, I wonder if people are pleased Salem Village has its own church. It was so delightful, seeing the church raised into a proper meetinghouse. Now, though, the reality of its close proximity to us all surely must be settling in. No longer must villagers make the ten-mile walk to Salem Town to attend meeting—but then again, they weren't expected to be present in town every week. Now everyone must participate in the village meeting or be fined.

Thomas Putnam, the Younger

September 1675
Salem Village Parade Ground

I walk down the ranks of the village militia, each filled with men I've known my entire life. Every man stands with his eyes facing forward, his flintlock held tightly to his side.

Ever since the Wampanoags took up arms against Plimoth, a sense of deadly seriousness pervades Saturday afternoon drills. I didn't quite understand why three Indians killing another Indian concerned the Plimoth court, even if the victim Sassamon was a converted, praying Indian. His death was of no concern to Plimoth. Clearly, the Wampanoag leader, King Philip, felt the same way. After the Plimoth court executed three Indians for Sassamon's murder, King Philip retaliated with an attack on Deerfield. Now the entire colony prepares for war.

"Shoulder arms!" I shout. Twenty men lift the flintlocks by their sides. "Fire by ranks to the forward. First rank to the forward. March!"

The first rank of four men marches forward.

"Present yer piece!"

The men lift their weapons to the firing position.

"Retire!"

The men return their weapons to shoulder arms and withdraw to the back of the ranks so the next rank can come forward.

After all ranks complete the drill, I give the command to order arms. The men stand at attention.

I walk back and forth in front of them with my hands clasped behind my back.

"Ye've done well, but not well enough. We lost seventy-four men at the recent battle at Bloody Brook, including Captain Lathrop. We lost these men because they were not alert to the enemy's surprise tactics. We will drill until ye can go through every required step without thought. When yer rank retires, ye will reload yer musket with a speed of four charges per minute. Prepare a bandolier to hold at least fifteen pouches of gunpowder so ye can reload quickly. Bring it with ye next week. As soon as we have sufficient supplies, we will fire our weapons." I infuse my voice with a dramatic pitch. "The enemy does not rest, and neither do we! He slithers and slides into forests and swamps, and we will root him out and destroy him."

I stop my pacing and raise my fist.

"Huzzah! Huzzah! Huzzah!" the men cheer.

I respond with a tight smile and motion for Lieutenant Ingersoll to take his position in front of the militia. Ingersoll moves from his viewing position outside his ordinary and makes his way to the front, where he silently faces the men for a moment before clearing his throat.

"I have a serious announcement," he begins. "Take heed. The Salem Militia Committee will meet shortly to determine who will join the Massachusetts Bay army and who will remain to defend Salem. Be prepared. If ye are pressed into service, ye leave for the assembly point *immediately*."

The men shift their feet.

"Attention!" I growl.

Ingersoll raises his hands. "I will sponsor the first round of ale at my ordinary. Sergeant Putnam, dismiss the men."

I return to my position and shout, "Dismissed!"

The men break ranks and walk the short distance to Ingersoll's Ordinary. I shake my head. Ingersoll might sponsor the first round of ale, but he'll make up the cost when the men order two or three more rounds.

Inside the tavern, I place my sword on one of the hooks by the door. The men's flintlocks lean on the wall, barrels facing up. I pass the bar to pick up my free ale and make my way to the back table, where my father and Ingersoll sit quietly, conversing. I clap my men on their shoulders as I pass, complimenting them on their drilling skills or their crops or anything else I can think of. When I reach the table, I turn my chair around so I can rest my arms on the back of it, take a long drink of ale, and wipe the back of my hand over my mouth.

"It's been a long afternoon," I comment.

"Ye've done well with the men," Father says. "I didn't think they would ever take drilling seriously."

"Losing seventy-four men at Bloody Brook got their attention," I reply, voice grim. Father does nothing but sigh and nod. In the gap of our exchange, the barman drops more tankards on the table and moves away.

"So, tell me," I say, "who sits on our militia committee?"

"It's filled with Salem Town men. William Hathorne, for one," Ingersoll responds. "But don't worry. The committee won't take eldest sons, even if they are unmarried."

I grunt. "Doesn't matter to me. I'm going to volunteer."

"What!?" Father spits out a mouthful of ale. I knew he'd react this way, hence why I've avoided this conversation for *weeks* now. "Ye're my eldest son and my heir! Why would ye consider such a thing?"

"Why not? Yer present wife prefers her own son for the position of heir," I blurt out—and, like a coward, I find I can't meet my father's eyes when I say it. "Besides, I'm not the kind of man to send village men into battle without someone to look out for them. I'm pretty sure most of the militia will stay here. Am I correct, Lieutenant Ingersoll?"

Ingersoll looks startled to have been called upon and clears his throat. "That's usually the case. Impressment allows us to select men who don't contribute to the community. Hired hands. Drifters. People who give nothing of importance to society."

I grin without humor. "Except, perhaps, to drink at yer ordinary."

"I'm not a man to turn away custom."

"Indeed. By the way, as lieutenant of our militia, will ye be answering the call for men?"

"Ye said it yerself. As an officer, it is my duty to see that the men are well trained. And now I have to elevate someone to sergeant rank."

I stand and knock my knuckles on the table. "Make it a temporary appointment. I'll want my billet back when I return. Come, Father. Yer wife doesn't like it when we're late for supper."

Thomas Putnam, the Younger

December 19, 1675
North Kingston, Rhode Island

The order comes down the line: "Fall in!"

I slip my bandolier across my chest, shoulder my knapsack with the few supplies I have left, and pick up my flintlock. Trudging through deep snow, I lead my men from Salem Village to their assigned rank.

"March!" someone shouts, and our ungainly Massachusetts army begins moving toward Pettaquamscut, where we will meet men from Connecticut.

I shiver in the predawn darkness, glad my unit isn't leading the army. Soldiers step where those ahead of them have left their footprints in the deep snow. Snow flurries fall all day, whipped up by a cold wind. The army marches through thick woods and wades across gullies, climbs hills and crosses frozen fields. The trek feels endless.

I think about the garrison where we hope to shelter out of the wind for the night. I fantasize about the potential of a cooking pot over a blazing fire. Hot soup, fresh ale. The opportunity to kick my feet up beside a crackling fire and perhaps even get some rest.

There is no point trying to hide from the Narragansetts who, considering all the noise we make, undoubtedly know we're coming.

The men reach the borders of the swamp, which has frozen due to the unusually cold weather, creating a spectacularly eerie setting. The trees, naked in winter, jet up like stakes from a sheet of frosted ice. A cloak of fog sinks from the sky, an oppressive force, and I suddenly get the feeling we are all being watched.

Eventually, we reach what was once a garrison. Now, it is a hollow remnant of the structure.

It isn't long before my boot snags something half-buried in the still-falling snow. I glance down and realize, with horror, that it's a body I've nearly tripped over. We count seventeen men in total, all slain in cold blood. How long ago, it is hard to say, given the weather.

A burial detail searches the men for identification and any useful supplies before digging shallow graves in the frozen earth.

I reach for my mother's locket. I keep the small piece of jewelry with its decorative filigree in a protective oilskin and carry it with me everywhere. I look around at this startling setting—with those frozen-stiff bodies being lugged away like lumber to shallow graves—and wonder if I'll join her in death soon. I'm too cold and hungry to care.

Perhaps it's the delirium of exhaustion and fear, but when I look at the locket and try to recall my mother's face, all I see is Ann Carr. I've taken her hand in mine many times—properly, respectfully. But I haven't ever felt the warm embrace of it upon my cheek. I realize now I'll stop at nothing to experience her in that way.

If I live through the battle, I'll ask her to marry me and give her the locket as a token. The thought gives me determination to survive.

I see a group of Salem villagers shivering under a small tent and join them.

"Sergeant," John Dodge says, alerting the men I'm among them.

I nod and think I should say something to encourage them, and yet the words don't emerge as quickly as they normally do. "Well," I begin, my voice a rasp, "we made it this far. It's in Jehovah's hands whether we survive the battle tomorrow, so pray for his blessing tonight. Tomorrow, stay alive, and kill as many Indians as ye can."

"Aye, Sergeant," one of the men says. "We'll do that if we don't freeze to death tonight."

A chuckle of despair passes over the group until all fall silent.

The next morning, a weak winter sun peeks through gray skies. When the signal to move out passes through the camp, men pack up their supplies and fall briefly into formation before separating to make their way through the forested swamp. Normally impassable, the frozen water creates a make-shift pathway.

The raised island in the middle of the swamp reveals a settlement surrounded by a double row of wooden palisades, a thick hedge, and a blockhouse. I always assumed Indians lived in caves and hovels like hibernating bears, but this is as formidable as any colonial fortress. There is no way to know how many warriors are within.

From what I can see, the only way to enter the camp is through an unfinished corner of the blockhouse, presently protected by logs. Massachusettsan companies led by Captains Moseley and Davenport lead the way.

Men slip and slide through snow and mud, their weapons banging against the ground. No sounds reach us from behind the palisade, and we don't know what to expect as men ahead of us push through the seemingly unprotected corner. When Moseley breaches the entry point, volleys of musket fire break out above him. *It's a trap!* The enemy is ready for our assault, not timidly hiding behind rocks and trees. *Has Jehovah abandoned us to our sinful fate?*

Moseley makes it through the rain of gunfire, as do many of Davenport's men. But Davenport himself falls at the entrance. Men pour around and over his corpse, pushing their way forward. I want to run, but there's nowhere to go, and the men behind me press our assault forward. Desperate, I raise my arm over my head to motion my men to follow me. I ignore Davenport's trampled body and the fallen men beside him and push into the fort.

Inside, the scene is a smoke-filled chaos of shouts, shots, screams, and sheer terror. Sparks fly from ignited powder. Air smelling of sulfur coats my throat and lungs while shadows dance in the hazy air. I think this must be hell, halfway expecting Lucifer to appear with his pitchfork.

I drop behind a wigwam to catch my breath. A drummer pounds out the sequence for loading and firing muskets. The sound pulls me away from my terror into the familiar drill. After withdrawing a pouch from my bandolier, I prime the breech with gunpowder, close the pan, ram the lead ball down the barrel, stand, take aim, and fire. It's like shooting waterfowl out of the sky. I mindlessly repeat the sequence. My ears ring until I'm deaf. My eyes water when I aim at the shapes in front of me. My skin burns from the overheated barrel. With no sense of time, I repeat the drill, sure that if I stop, I shall die.

Prime. Ram. Aim. Fire. Prime. Ram. Aim. Fire.

All the while, snow falls, blending with spilled blood to become a pink, slushy substance on the ground. In the oncoming darkness, the surviving Indians flee into the forest. Bodies from both sides litter the fort.

Someone hands me a torch. "Major Appleton's orders! Burn it all!"

I swipe at a food storage area and several wigwams before passing the torch to someone else. Fire swirls across the fortress, creating a five-acre inferno that looks like a lower level of hell. I wonder if those who fled the flames will be able to survive this winter weather. My lips shift into a vicious snarl. The Indians should have thought of that before they raided settlements and farms. Before they killed my countrymen. Before they took me to the gates of hell.

For the second time on this endless day, I prepare to move out with my men. We left for the Great Swamp before dawn. Now it is dusk. After checking to be sure my wounded friend Thomas Flint is secured onto a loose horse, I guide the gelding onto the road that leads out of the swamp and on to Wickford. My clothes, caked with blood, freeze on my body. Wind batters our progress. But we keep walking until the army finally reaches its destination. I pull Flint off the horse and carry him to a shelter where a fire can warm him and surgeons can treat him. Finding a spot slightly sheltered from the wind, I collapse onto the ground and sleep.

Ann Carr

Late February 1676
Putnam House, Salem Village

I stand just out of view at the entrance to the Putnam's main room but haven't the courage to enter. There is a whisper of spring in the air, and I want to share this promise of renewal with Tom. He sits in front of the fire with his back to me. I take a breath and enter the room.

Though the weather has warmed slightly, Tom slouches before a blazing fire on a straight-backed armchair with his legs stretched out in front of him. Heat from the hearth suffocates the room. I take off my shawl and sit on a bench away from the flames.

"Mistress Carr, is that ye?" he asks while keeping his gaze on the fire.

"Yes, Master Putnam." I clear my throat. He does not meet my eyes and continues to stare, as though hypnotized. "I came to see if ye might like to walk outside. The crocuses are blooming. And I thought a bit of fresh air might do ye good. Ye haven't left the house since yer return six weeks ago."

"Have ye ever looked into a fire, Mistress Carr?" Tom asks, and I brace myself. He's pinned me with these impossible questions ever since the battle in December. "Looked at it deeply enough to see colors dance in the flames? Sometimes, if ye look closely, ye can see shapes. Such a curious thing, fire. It both warms . . . and destroys."

"I'm sure someone could tend the fire for a bit until it dies down, and ye could come out with me." *Please.*

"I've been to church," Tom mumbles. "That must count for something."

"I'm sure it does. Um . . . I brought ye a gift."

"Oh? What is it, then? Show me."

I feel suddenly shy. "It isn't much. Just a pair of gloves. I had some extra wool, and when ye returned, ye mentioned how cold yer hands were. So I made ye these gloves."

I reach into my pocket and pull out a pair of thick fingerless gloves. Even now, Tom can't seem to find it in himself to look away from the flames.

"I thought ye'd need yer fingers free for . . . um . . . loading yer musket, I suppose."

"What do ye know about muskets?"

I shake my head. "Nothing, really. I just used to watch when ye drilled the militia, and it seemed like ye needed to use yer fingers."

I walk over to Tom's chair and hand him the gloves.

Tom strokes the wool before pulling the gloves over his hands. He looks back at the fire and then turns his attention to me, at last. "These are wonderful. If only I had them on the campaign. I've never been so cold."

"I'm sorry I didn't give them to ye before ye left. Do ye like them?"

"Very much. Thank ye." His eyes, at first soft, turn suddenly wild. "Do ye know what kept me going when I was cold and afraid?"

"Ye would never be afraid," I whisper, trying to counteract his mood.

"Ah, but I was." He lets this hang in the air, as oppressive as the heat. I see his throat bob and wonder what words he's just choked back. "I thought I would die from the cold, or the Indians would kill me with their tomahawks. A military campaign isn't the same as a drill."

I do not reply, for I know the question is rhetorical.

"In a drill, there is no enemy," Tom says. "In a campaign, enemies surround ye, but ye don't know where they are, exactly. Ye can't see them through the smoke or flames, but ye hear their bloodthirsty cries."

"I cannot imagine," I say, taken aback.

Tom glances back at the fire. "How old are ye now?"

"Ye asked me that almost three years ago, when we buried my niece. Do ye remember?"

Tom tapped his chin. "I do. Ye were twelve years old then."

I smile. "And that makes me fifteen years old now."

"Still too young."

"For?"

"Never mind." Tom stands and reaches into the pocket in his breeches. I watch him withdraw a small package covered in oilskin. "Open yer hand," he says.

I hold out my right hand with my palm facing up.

Tom folds my fingers over the package. "Look and see what's inside."

I sit down at the table and carefully unwrap three layers of oilskin until I reach a soft wool wrapping that conceals a small gold locket.

"It's beautiful."

"It is," Tom agrees. "It was my mother's. There's a lock of her hair inside if ye care to open it."

I don't know if he wants me to open the locket or not. Maybe he's being polite? Or maybe he wants to share something precious with me. I open the clasp. Inside, I see a small lock of light-brown hair tied with string. I catch my breath. Tom is sharing something precious with me, a part of himself no one else knows.

"It is beautiful, Tom." I close the locket and begin rewrapping the wool. "Thank ye for sharing it with me—"

"No. Ye don't understand." He pushes my hand back. "My mother brought the locket with her from England. She wore it always to remember her home. When she lay dying, she gave it to me and told me to keep it safe. To give it to someone I care for."

I have to force my jaw not to drop. *He's giving it to me. He cares for me.*

"I've kept it hidden and safe ever since. When I was shivering—from the cold, of course—I held my mother's locket between my fingers and thought of ye. Memories of ye and my mother gave me the courage to live. I want ye to keep the locket and wear it always." This time, he rests a hand over my own, the locket tucked inside my grip. He gives me a meaningful look. "In two years, I'll ask ye a question that will change both of our lives."

I realize now this isn't just a gift—it's a promise.

I unwrap the locket again and hold the necklace open so Tom can fasten it for me. I hear him breathe as he closes the clasp. He squeezes my shoulders. I could faint from his nearness.

"Wear the locket under yer clothing, or else there might be questions we don't want to answer."

I smile, touch the locket, and drop it under my fichu.

Ann Carr

June 1678
Salem Village Parsonage

Shading my eyes from the afternoon sun, I can barely see the village training field. I'm near enough to see men completing the drill to load and fire but too far away to recognize any man in particular.

Even so, I can guess which one is Tom Putnam. He's the only man moving through the ranks while the others remain in formation. The slight smile on my face turns into a scowl as my brother-in-law approaches.

"Is there a reason ye're standing idle when there is so much to be done?" he asks.

"Mary told me to get some fresh air, but I didn't want to go too far, lest I'm needed."

"Which is why ye must go back inside. This time of day, the children are probably hungry. Please attend them. I'll be upstairs."

"Yes, Reverend Bayley."

I nod to the nursemaid, a new girl named Rebecca, and separate James and Sarah, who seem to be squabbling over a ball. Between us, we usher the two toddlers into the kitchen and settle them in raised chairs, each with a tray in front. Both children begin bouncing their legs against the chairs.

"Come, Mary Ann," I call to the oldest child. "Time to eat."

When she sits at the table, I place a bowl of porridge in front of her and hand her a wooden spoon. Then I take bowls over to the high chairs and give each child a spoon. James and Sarah are less interested in eating than in making designs in the gooey porridge. I pick up their spoons and begin feeding them while the nursemaid looks after Mary Ann.

Juggling the spoons, I blow a loose hair off my face. Someone bangs the door knocker.

I give the spoons back to James and Sarah.

"Do not make a mess," I order and tuck my hair under my coif. *Pity Reverend Bayley is too busy to answer the door of his own house.*

When I pull the door open, Tom Putnam stands before me in his uniform. "Oh!"

"Mistress Carr, have I come at an awkward time? We haven't crossed paths in a long time, and I thought with the new babe being a month old, it would be acceptable to call."

"Yes. Yes, of course. Come into the front room." I smooth down my apron and pick up an errant toy, leading the way into the room. "May I get ye something? Small beer, perhaps?"

Tom stands awkwardly, clutching a hat in his hands. He's aged since he returned from the Indian war. When he issues orders to the militia, his voice is harsher. His stance radiates brute strength. And his eyes have more depth, as if they can look through a person.

"Please sit." *I feel flustered in his presence.* "I'll get the beer."

I dart back into the kitchen, startling Rebecca.

"I'm sorry," I say to her. "Ye'll have to finish up with the children on yer own. Sergeant Putnam is here. Can ye look and see if I have a smudge on my face? It feels like Sarah marked me."

Rebecca takes the cloth she was using to clean up the children and wipes my cheek. "Ye're fine now. I'll take the children upstairs."

I make a tray with two tankards and a pitcher of beer and return to the front room.

Tom sits with his elbows on his knees and a pensive look on his face.

I pour out the beer and hand Tom a tankard.

"Thank ye. Um. I brought something for the baby," he says, reaching into his pocket to retrieve a wooden baby rattle with small bells attached.

"It's charming. My sister will be so pleased. How have ye been? I haven't seen much of ye these past few months."

Tom clears his throat. "I've been building a house on land my father gave me."

My stomach plummets. *If Tom is building a house, he must plan to share it with someone. Is that why he's acting so strange? Why he's been so distant? I think of two years ago, the locket he'd given me, the promise he'd made. Was that all for naught?*

"Ye have?" I ask weakly.

Tom spreads out his calloused hands. "Yes. At the moment, I just have the box frame up with the second-floor overhang. I plan to add the lean-to at the back later, but I want to smooth out the interior first."

I sip my beer and place the tankard on the small table between the straight-backed chairs.

"It sounds like ye've been busy."

"Well, it's time for me to marry—"

Marry?

"—so I need to prepare a house."

I don't know what to say. "Do ye still have difficulty sleeping?" I blurt out, of all things.

Tom looks bewildered by my question. "I'm ashamed to say I do. Why do ye ask?"

"No reason," I say, smiling with embarrassment. *Stop speaking, Ann!*

"Yes, well—"

"I still have yer locket," I blurt out next. I find I'd rather talk about anything *except* Tom's probable engagement. Surely that's what he's about to announce. I pull the delicate chain out from under my fichu and confess, "I never take it off."

The tension in Tom's shoulder eases.

"I came to—"

I hear the sound of feet pounding down the stairs, and my brother-in-law appears with a broad smile and an outstretched hand. "Sergeant Putnam! *Tom,*" he says warmly. It's the sort of warmth he's never shown me. "I didn't know ye came to call, for I wasn't informed. I was in my study when I heard voices." He gives me a disapproving look. "Ann, ye should have informed me when Sergeant Putnam arrived."

I drop my eyes, embarrassed for Tom to see how my brother-in-law disregards me.

"How may I be of service, Sergeant Putnam?"

"I merely stopped by to invite Mistress Carr to view the new house I'm building on my father's homestead. I . . ." Tom clears his throat. "I wanted a woman's opinion before I begin working with the interior space."

"What a splendid idea. We can make a party of it. It's time Mistress Bayley had an outing, and I'm very interested in plans for yer farm. Shall we say Tuesday next after nooning?"

No! If Tom meets me alone, we can talk, and he'll realize I'm a better partner for him than whoever he's courting. Is he courting? Maybe he isn't. Or maybe—

Tom glances at the locket he gave me before turning his gaze back to his host. Catching his eye, I slip the necklace under a fold near my neckline.

Reverend Bayley waits for Tom's reply, as if viewing an unfinished house is the height of entertainment.

I hold Tom's gaze. "I look forward to seeing yer new house," I say, inserting myself firmly into Tom's invitation before my brother-in-law can push me out.

"Next week Tuesday, then." Tom looks at me with what could be a slight smile. "Shall ye make yer way across?"

My brother-in-law answers before I can reply. "Of course. It's not very far. Come, Sergeant Putnam. I'll stand ye a round at Ingersoll's Ordinary. Ann, please tell my wife I will return shortly."

As Reverend Bayley strides out the door, Tom stands. "I'm sorry, Mistress. That is not how I hoped to issue the invitation. But I'm pleased ye will see the house. I hope that ye will eventually spend a fair amount of time there. I wish ye good day."

"And to ye," I reply.

He hopes I'll spend a fair amount of time at his house. What can he mean? The possibility is too much to consider—dare I hope he thinks of me fondly after all?

Ann Carr

Tuesday
Salem Village Parsonage

My sister kisses her baby and hands her off to Rebecca. The pair of them stroll out into the kitchen, leaving my sister and me to ourselves.

My sister secures her new hat on her head. "What do ye think, Ann? Do I look like a proper minister's wife?"

I raise my eyebrows. "What a strange question. Ye *are* the minister's wife."

"Yes, but it's my first time outside the parsonage since John was born last month. I'm excited to leave the house. Do ye have the basket of food?"

"Why are we taking food? We're just going to see Sergeant Putnam's new house."

Mary links her arm around mine and leads me outside. "Ye really don't know, do ye?" she says with a grin. "How is that possible?"

"What do ye mean?"

"Why do ye think Sergeant Putnam wants ye to see the house?"

I blink against the bright sunlight and adjust my hat. "He wants our opinion before he shows the house to a woman who has caught his eye," I say, feeling put out. At first, I'd wanted to spend time with Tom and see his property. I thought I might persuade him I would be the perfect wife for him. But now I know that is wishful thinking on my part and find I'd rather not see his house at all. "He said it's time for him to marry, so he must have someone in mind."

"I'm sure he does," Mary says. "Let's wait a moment outside the meetinghouse. Reverend Bayley will join us here, and we'll walk across the field together."

I pick a few sprigs of milkweed near the meetinghouse and begin twisting them together into a posey for my sister. "Why is Reverend Bayley coming with us?"

"Ye don't think he wants to spend time with me?"

"I do not," I say honestly.

"Yer answer is a bit harsh, but sadly correct," my sister surprises me by saying. "The reverend is concerned about divisions in the village . . ."

"Divisions?"

Mary sighs, then lowers her voice. "There is a strong faction that opposes the Putnam family, and they are targeting my husband. Reverend Bayley says he might lose his church, and *then* where will we be? He's hoping this will give him a chance to find out more about Deacon Putnam's thoughts on the matter. Also, his presence means there will be no gossip about ye."

I turn to face Mary. "Gossip? Why would anyone gossip?"

"Be serious, Ann. This village is nothing but gossip. Men's stories. Women's tales."

My hand clenches around the posey. "Oh, dear. I made a posey for ye, and now I've crushed it."

Reverend Bayley emerges from the meetinghouse and offers his right arm to his wife and his left to me. "Shall we be off, then?"

Mary and I find ourselves walking two steps for each of Reverend Bayley's strides.

"Please, slow down, Reverend Bayley," Mary pants. "This is my first visit outside the house, and Ann has the basket to carry."

Reverend Bayley shoots me an annoyed glance.

"Forgive me," he says and slows his pace but only for a short while.

By the time we reach Tom's homestead, sweat slips down my face and strands of my hair stick to my forehead. The house is a simple structure. Two stories and a large chimney. A central door. Diamond-paned windows.

"Sergeant Putnam!" Reverend Bayley calls out. "We're here at last."

Tom looks up from the raised garden frames he's assembling. He puts down his mallet and rubs his hands on his trousers before coming forward.

I smile in anticipation.

"Mistress Carr, I'm pleased to see ye," Tom says. "Please, let me take the basket."

"Thank ye," I say, extending it to him. He takes it and offers me his arm.

"We can leave it in the shade while ye view the house," he says.

My cheeks heat with excitement.

"Come, everyone, let us go inside, and ye can give me ideas for finishings," Tom goes on, escorting us all—with me on his arm—to the entryway. "The exteriors will weather over the summer if it pleases Jehovah. But it would be good to have some color inside."

Entering the house, I note the sturdy oak logs that support the second level. *It would be wonderful to live here. Snug in winter.*

"Such a large hearth!" Mary exclaims.

"I like a large hearth," Tom said. "I was a bit extravagant with the brick-work. I used my bonus from the war to pay for it, but I thought my future wife might appreciate a bit of decoration. What do ye think, Mistress Carr?"

Why do I have to approve of things he made for someone else?

"It's lovely," I comment while keeping my expression neutral.

"And a color for the walls? What do ye think? Maybe a warm tone? If we leave the walls as they are, they will probably look like soot before winter arrives."

"I didn't know ye like colors."

"There are probably lots of things about me ye don't know . . . yet."

What does he mean by that?

"Reverend Bayley," Mary said. "May I trouble ye to look at the frames Sergeant Putnam is building? I think I would like something similar for the parsonage."

"Ye can tell the outside man what ye want."

"But I want *ye* to walk with me. Please."

"Yes, please walk about the garden area. I'd be pleased to have yer opinion," Tom says.

Mary pulls her husband's arm, and he reluctantly acquiesces. "Very well, Mistress Bayley. I shall escort ye."

The door snicks shut.

I walk further into the room. The windows let in more light than I expected.

I've never been truly alone with Tom before. I feel slightly dizzy as if I'm floating. Tom looks at me expectantly. "Um . . . what sort of colors are ye considering?"

"I thought perhaps something reddish," Tom replies.

I walk around the edges of the room, pretending to consider possible colors. I wish I could live here with Tom, enjoying the sun streaming through the window and playing with our children. I touch the locket nestled under my fichu. I should give it back. Tom will never marry me. I was a fool to think he would consider me.

I turn to look at Tom and take a deep breath to steady myself.

"Forgive me for my impertinence," I whisper, "but who did ye build this house for? Who caught yer eye?"

Tom reaches his hand out to touch my shoulder. "Ye don't know?" he says in a choked voice.

"If I did, I wouldn't ask."

Tom squeezes my shoulder. He stands so close to me I can see his pupils. "It's *ye*," he murmurs. "It's always been ye. From the day ye arrived in the village, I knew ye would be my wife, but I had to wait for ye to grow up. And now, by my reckoning, ye are seventeen years old."

"Aye, I am." My voice sounds like a breathy whisper.

Tom steps back and lifts my hand. "So now I can ask for yer hand in marriage. If I ask, will ye give it to me?"

I nod, unable to speak. Tears of joy stream down my cheeks.

"Mistress Ann Carr," Tom says, "will ye join yer life to mine? Will ye live in this house with me? Will ye bear our children?"

"I will," I gasp. "Yes. Oh, yes!"

Tom cups my face. "Before the others return," he whispers, "may I kiss ye?"

"Yes," I breathe.

My heart pounds as if it will explode. Tom takes my hands and draws me closer. Closer. When his lips brush mine, I feel like I'm floating. I feel free and sheltered and safe.

All too soon, the others return, and Tom steps away from me. He doesn't mention our conversation. His father and my brother-in-law have to draw up the marriage contract. But we are plighted to each other, and I've never felt so happy.

CHAPTER

Ann Carr Putnam

February 1679
Salem Village Parsonage

My sister is heavily pregnant with her seventh child. Each pregnancy takes more out of her, as if the babes, in their innocence, leach her life force. Her nine-month-old son John squirms in my lap until I hand him a piece of hard bread to calm him. He has teeth now, so Mary took her breast away and replaced it with pap—a gooey concoction her children throw onto the floor as often as they eat it. Watching them smearing breakfast across their little faces makes me queasy.

"Ye look piqued," Mary says. "Are ye ill?"

She peruses my face before pointedly looking at my belly.

"Do ye think anyone is in yer womb? There should be by now. How are things between ye and Sergeant Putnam?"

Baby John's spit covers my hand. I pretend to fuss with wiping it clean, averting my eyes from my sister's inquisitions. She is my dearest sister, but I find I can't tell her the truth. My husband is a man tormented. During the day, he is a whirl of activity. We have one laborer less than we should, so he can work the fields and nurture our livestock himself. He allows me to supervise our garden but not to aerate the soil. Again, this he does himself, at my direction. Once a week, he drills the militia. But otherwise, he keeps away from the village no matter how much his father urges him to participate in its affairs.

At night, Tom holds me close as he sweats out his dreams, but he will not speak of them. On the rare days I press him, he gets that strange look in his eyes—the same strange, hypnotic look he once had while staring at the flames in the hearth. He says he's just a fitful sleeper. Some mornings, he reaches for me. Others, he is up and away to the meadow or the barn or any place I am not.

"They are well," I lie. "My husband is a good man, a good provider."

"And *ye*?" she prods.

I bob my chin for emphasis. "In full health," I assure her, but she doesn't look convinced.

Mary shifts her bulk and leans over my chair to sniff my breath before returning to her seat.

She gives me a knowing look. "Did ye puke this morning? Or last week? And all the mornings in between?"

"Yes," I whisper, embarrassed. I hold a hand up to my mouth. "Yes to everything ye asked. What's wrong with me?"

"I think ye know." Mary laughs at my discomfort. "It means all will be well with ye, and soon the babe on yer knee will be yers, not mine. It won't be official until ye feel her move, but I've gone through this enough to recognize the signs."

"I was afraid . . ."

"Nonsense." Mary pats my hand and gives me a rueful smile. "Now ye've started, ye'll be like me and never stop. It's best if ye keep it our secret until ye feel her moving, though."

I nod, opening my mouth to say more, but am interrupted by my brother-in-law, who comes through the front door with my husband's father. Reverend Bayley kisses his wife's cheek before addressing me. "Ann, I didn't expect to see ye here, though I know my wife appreciates yer assistance. She's been lonely since ye married."

"Hush, Reverend Bayley," Mary says. "She visits me most days at times when ye are out in the parish. What brings ye home now?"

"Deacon Putnam and I have things to discuss. Sit down, Deacon Putnam. Ann, since ye're here, make us some tea, please."

The men take seats in the front room near the fire while I pour water from the ever-boiling kettle on the kitchen hearth into a porcelain teapot; Reverend Bayley likes to demonstrate his social standing before men like the Putnams. I take a tray to the table between the chairs near the fire. Mary lowers herself slowly onto the bench at the edge of the room and leans her back against the wall. I pour her some tea and sit beside her.

"I fear my disagreement with Bray Wilkins has become something much greater than it should have," Reverend Bayley begins. "I've served the church and the village for six years without any disagreements. Clearly, Jehovah is testing me in some way. Perhaps I should resign."

He rubs his hand on the back of his neck in a rare display of self-doubt.

Mary presses her lips together and strokes her belly.

"No," my father-in-law says. "Jehovah has nothing to do with this. The issue is a grab for power by the Porters and their supporters. They think they're better than those of us who work the land. But we built Salem Town's backwater of farms into a functioning village. They know they cannot best us, so they seek to humiliate us by claiming we called ye to the pulpit without following proper procedures. If they prevail, they will put their own man in yer place. Ye must stand firm, Reverend Bayley. Ye cannot bend the knee to their claims. Ye were called by a general consent and vote of every person in the village, as was legal and binding."

"I do not wish to stay where I am not wanted."

Deacon Putnam waves his hand in dismissal and pulls a letter out from under his coat. Mary leans forward, her eyes glued to the parchment.

"What is that?" Reverend Bayley asks.

"This," Deacon Putnam says with a note of triumph, "is the General Court's judgment on this issue. They note that the court authorized the inhabitants to call a preacher. They recognize ye as orthodox and blameless and note the majority in our village want ye to stay in the pulpit. They extend yer position for a year while we work things out with the Porters. Make no mistake, they shall rue the day they moved against us."

Mary squeezes my hand. "I've been so worried," she whispers. "I thought we would be cast out." Tears run down her cheeks. Wrapped up in the bliss of my marriage, I gave no thought to her worries. *How could I have been so callous?*

Ann Carr Putnam

March 1679
Salem Village Parsonage

Mary stumbles a bit as I walk her around the room. Her lying-in is in the parlor since it's the warmest room in the house.

"Set her in the birthing chair," the midwife says.

As soon as she's settled in the chair, the midwife reaches under my sister's shift. I take an extra interest compared to Mary's previous births, because I'm pretty sure my sister was right last month. I puke most days and hardly keep food down. Even my husband mentioned it. I told him it was the change of weather, and he didn't press me.

I hold a cup of ale to her lips. Mary squirms in discomfort.

The midwife reaches back under her shift. "The babe is ready. Push!"

My sister shrieks so loudly the men must hear it at Ingersoll's Ordinary. For the first time, I realize Mary's agony will soon be my own. Will Jehovah take my first child like he did Mary's? I couldn't bear it. This is Mary's seventh child. Seven! Each bringing her discomfort and hours of agony as she pushes them out of her body.

I wipe Mary's brow and whisper words of encouragement while she shrieks and moans.

"Push!" the midwife orders, holding out her hands.

"Now! Push hard!"

Mary shrieks. The midwife catches the slippery infant.

"Ye have a son," she says in triumph and slaps his bottom.

The babe cries as I take him to wash and swaddle before bringing him back to my sister, who cuddles and coos at her newest son.

"Jehovah has made me the living mother of another living child," she murmurs. "Blessed be Jehovah."

I hold a cup of caudle to her lips so she can drink without disturbing the infant.

"Have ye decided on a name?" the midwife asks.

"Samuel, because Jehovah hears us."

Ann Carr Putnam

March 1679

Ingersoll's Ordinary

My brother-in-law stands with Deacon Putnam on his left side and Deacon Ingersoll on his right. His pale face is pinched in discomfort. My husband guides me through the raucous assembly to join them on the far side of the tavern with Reverend Bayley's other supporters. Unlike the dissenters, they nurse their tankards of ale in almost complete silence.

"Look at them," my husband mutters. "We live in harmony all these years until the Porters decide to take what is ours. It is pathetic."

One of Deacon Ingersoll's servants brings a tray with tankards of ale to the table where the Putnams and their supporters sit with grim expressions and passes them around. The atmosphere is hostile and filled with tension.

"Mistress Putnam, how pleasant to see ye again." I extend my hand across the table to my mother-in-law.

"Yes," she replies without changing her stern expression. "And how is yer sister? Recovering well, I hope."

"As well as can be expected in all this turmoil. She'll receive visitors in a few weeks."

Mistress Putnam nods and briefly glances at my husband. Before she can speak again, Deacon Ingersoll raps on the bar for attention and calls the meeting to order.

"It is disappointing," he begins, "that even after the General Court ruling that the procedures for calling Reverend Bayley were correct, and that he should remain with us, there are those among us who still call for his dismissal."

Master Porter stands with his hands in his pockets. He rocks back on his heels.

"We do not accept the ruling," he says in an even voice, "and appeal to the church at Salem to settle the matter."

My brother-in-law seems to shrink before my eyes, and who could blame him? This is a matter that is only worsening. I cannot fathom how it'll be improved. I look to my father-in-law, gauging his reaction, and am startled to see that Deacon Putnam looks as if he would like to cross the tavern floor to attack Master Porter.

"Porter cares nothing about the church, only about seizing control of the village from us," my husband mutters before dropping his head. "Ann, I'm sorry for ye to witness such petty, selfish concerns. In yer condition, ye need calm."

"My condition?"

"I have eyes and many siblings." He touches my hand before returning his attention to his ale.

Is he pleased I may carry his child? I can't tell from his expression.

"I have three petitions to read," Deacon Ingersoll says, "and ask for a show of hands in support of each. Master Porter, shall ye also take a count of hands?"

"With pleasure," Master Porter replies, sneering.

"The first petition states that Reverend Bayley was improperly called to our pulpit, because he was not called by church members only but by all inhabitants of the village. If ye agree, raise yer hands."

My husband groans as a series of hands shoot up toward the ceiling. I cannot tell if they're the majority, but it's close.

"Keep them up," Master Porter says.

The two men count for several minutes while my husband growls.

"I see sixteen hands," Master Porter says in a satisfied voice.

"Agreed." Deacon Ingersoll writes a note. "Now, the second petition is for Reverend Bayley to continue in his position as minister to the church in Salem Village in accordance with the General Court's verdict. Those in favor raise yer hands."

My husband rises to join in tallying the hands. With relief, I can tell already that the hands in favor of my brother-in-law's position appear to outweigh those against him. He, Deacon Ingersoll, and Master Porter count twice.

"I show thirty-nine hands," Deacon Ingersoll says. "Do ye agree, Master Porter?"

After a long pause, Master Porter nods his head and spits out his answer. "Agreed."

I exhale with relief.

"And, finally, I ask people here today who are not part of our village but attend meetings with us, if they agree with the General Court's verdict."

It looks like everyone present from outside our village raises their hands.

"That's ten more in favor of Reverend Bayley," Deacon Ingersoll announces. "I shall send the documents and the results of this meeting to Reverend Higginson at Salem Church and request their opinion on the matter, since our church falls under their jurisdiction. Reverend Bayley, please send us forth with a prayer."

My brother-in-law—whose face still looks pallid, albeit relieved—takes a position between the two factions and begins praying for harmony and peace within the village.

"No chance of that," my husband mutters.

I put my hand on his arm to calm him as his father approaches.

"Son." Deacon Putnam puts his hand out, but my husband ignores the gesture. Jaw tightening, he withdraws his hand, stowing it in his pocket. "Come to ours for supper."

"Thank ye for the invitation, but no. My wife and I will make our way home."

"I'm glad ye came today to stand with the family."

My husband turns to face his father. "I will always stand with our family, but in truth, the Porters are correct. I was at the meeting when ye all decided among yerselves to call Reverend Bayley. Ye controlled everything in the village between ye. Times change, and the fact that the General Court ruled in yer favor will not stop the dissent. Ye need to loosen yer grip."

To my shock, Deacon Putnam's eyes turn angry. He looks at my husband the same way he'd looked at Master Porter moments ago, as though he'd like to bridge the gap between himself and his target, launching an attack. "Ye would turn yer back on us?"

"Never," Tom reassures him. "But for now, I shall take my wife home. Good day to ye."

Tom puts his hand at my elbow and escorts me out of the tavern and onto the road. We don't speak on the walk home, but my mind whirls.

Will they put my brother-in-law out of his living? What will happen to my sister?

Mary and I have been together since I was born. If she is pushed out of her home, what will happen to us?

Reverend John Higginson

April 1679
Salem Town

Sitting at my favorite table—the one positioned just right to catch afternoon light from a nearby window—I place my pen and inkwell at a point convenient to the parchment awaiting my signed conclusion about the controversy in Salem Village.

With my elbows on the table, I steeple my hands, staring at the pen, inkwell, and parchment before me.

None of this has to do with church business; this is all local, political squabbling.

It was a mistake to allow the villagers to have their own church. They aren't intelligent enough to appreciate their good fortune. But the General Court gave them leave to call a nonordained minister, and now factions split the village. Reverend Bayley is a good man, but if he leaves, the villagers will eventually find fault with his replacement, and so it will go.

Sighing, I dip my pen into the ink and begin writing. *After much discussion, members of the church at Salem conclude that those in dissent regarding Reverend Bayley must submit to the generality who desire him to continue without any further trouble.*

I wonder if they will accept our ruling. Probably not. What a waste of time.

The General Court permitted Salem Village to call a minister not just to the notion of church members but to the entire number of inhabitants. Those who wish to see a separate church in the village should join the church in Salem, and when there are enough competent people to have their own church, they may call a minister according to the order of the gospel and the law of the General Court.

I sprinkle sand over the parchment to set the ink, fold the letter, and address it to the church committee at Salem Village. I cannot deter those determined to sow discord, but perhaps this will slow them down.

Thomas Putnam, the Younger

October 1679
Outside Tom Putnam's House

I put down my axe and pause to wipe my brow. I started splitting logs at sunrise, when the first midwife arrived, and now it's well past nooning.

How does my wife do? Will Jehovah spare her?

Every time the door opens, I hope for news my child is born. But the only information I learn is how many women are needed to assist my wife. Two midwives. My sister-in-law. Even my stepmother is in attendance, with three of her servants. Ann must be terrified to have so many women fussing around her.

I set another log on the stump and raise my axe again.

"How now?" a male voice calls.

I glance up to see my brother-in-law striding toward me.

"Reverend Bayley, what brings ye here?"

My brother-in-law slaps my shoulder. "I thought it well to see how ye are bearing up. I remember my wife's lying-in with our first babe. The hours seemed endless." Reverend Bayley looks at the stack of firewood. "I see ye found a way to pass the time."

I attempt to smile. "I'm aware of the devil's use for idle hands. Would ye care to come inside for refreshment?"

"In a moment," he says, expression growing solemn. "But first I thought to apprise ye of the General Court's decision about my enemies' latest petition and my response to it."

I stiffen. Whatever the General Court decrees, I'm wise enough to realize it won't stop those opposed to my wife's brother-in-law.

"What did the court rule?" I ask.

"The magistrates upheld their prior decision that until the village has a regular church, all inhabitants may call a minister. Yer father and the other deacons are pleased with this result, though it changes nothing."

"And ye?"

"I am not pleased," he says bluntly. "I refuse to spend my life being vilified for political reasons. I am stepping down at the turn of the new year."

So the victory will be against my father.

"Have ye told my father yer decision?"

"Not yet. Ye are the first to know. But once I tell my wife, she will tell her sister. I thought ye should break the news to yer good lady. She's been a bit fanciful of late. It may be well for ye to tell her first."

"Aye." I shrug into my jacket but don't bother to button it. We won't be going far. "The last month has been difficult. Come, Reverend, let us share a few tankards of ale."

Just as we reach the door, Mary Bayley opens it. Her eyes find her husband. "Oh! Reverend Bayley, I didn't expect to see ye here."

"I had news to share with Sergeant Putnam," he explains, pursing his lips. "And I wanted to see how events progress here."

Mary nods, then turns to me. "I was just coming to summon the new father. Sergeant Putnam, ye have a bonny daughter and an exhausted wife. Both are eager to see ye."

The tension leaves my body, and I sag with relief. Much like my wife, I haven't forgotten that terrible day we'd buried Mary's firstborn child; I've been haunted by it ever since, along with the desperate fear of losing Ann.

I take the stairs two at a time before pausing at our open bedroom door.

"Come in, come in." The midwife motions me forward. "Meet yer new daughter."

I cross the dim room to Ann's bedside, where she nurses our babe. She has deep shadows under her eyes but seems oddly content.

I kiss her fingers.

"How are ye, dear wife?"

"Relieved Jehovah spared us both. Next time, I'm sure we'll have a son."

Ann pulls back the edge of the swaddling linen, revealing my daughter's small face. Gazing at the tiny bundle, my heart swells.

"We'll call her Ann, after ye," I whisper in awe. "And I shall never love a son better than I love her."

CHAPTER

Ann Carr Putnam

Spring 1682
Salem Village Parsonage

I secure baby Thomas's arms as he roots into my breast and latches on.

"Ouch!" I wince.

"Feeding is a challenge when their teeth come in," Mary says in commiseration, shifting her own babe. "Fortunately, Isaac's teeth haven't come in yet."

We watch our joint herd of small children running through the house and out the door.

Mary sighs. "There's no controlling them until we strap them in the wagon later this morning. Yer Ann will miss her cousins, I'm sure."

At once, it's as though my heart breaks anew. My worst fears are coming true: My sister leaves today, and for the first time in my life, we're to be separated. "Not as much as I'll miss ye. Must ye leave us?" I ask again, holding back tears. "I don't know how I'll exist without ye."

Mary pats my hand, tears flooding her eyes as well.

"Ye know if I had a choice, we would stay here, but Reverend Bayley's mind is made up. He says he cannot watch factions continue to fracture the church he still loves."

"But why Killingworth? It's so far away. And the Putnams gave him enough land to farm here and be prosperous."

"Prosperity doesn't interest him. His calling is to serve Jehovah. And since he can't serve the church here, he will go where he can be of use."

I give way to sobbing again, and Mary detaches Isaac from her breast and puts him in a Moses basket so that she can cradle me instead. Me, her little sister—her first baby, in many ways.

"Come, dearest. The last boxes are gone," she says, whispering into my hairline as we embrace for what might be the last time. I can't bear to think of it. "It's time to put the children in the wagon and say farewell."

"No, I won't—I can't bear the thought of ye so far away," I tell her. "And ye carry another babe. Ye shouldn't go on such a long journey. Stay until the babe is born. Let yer husband go, and ye can bide with us."

I cling to Mary's arm when she tries to stand.

"Let go," Mary says, "lest ye drop yer babe."

I detach Thomas and shift him onto my hip. "I've done as ye asked. Now, tell me ye will stay here with—"

Reverend Bayley comes into the house and shoos his oldest children out the door. "Wife, it's time to say farewell. Everyone waits outside. Ye and Mistress Putnam can bring the younger children outside." He gives my sister a meaningful look that quite clearly conveys he will not tolerate any more delay.

On his heels, my sister follows, whisked away before I can beg her not to go. I follow miserably along in her wake, met at once with the cold drizzle of spring.

"All right, ye two," Reverend Bayley says, standing beside the wagon with his two oldest children. "When I boost ye up, find yer seat."

"It's not too late." I clutch my sister's hand. "Please, Mary, stay with me."

Mary looks at me with disapproval. "Ann, ye must stop this foolishness. We're grown women with families. My husband is removing to Killingworth, and I am going with him. Stop acting like a child."

A child! Can't she see how much I need her love?

I look at my daughter, who stands with Mary's children. "Ann Putnam, take my hand. Yer cousins are leaving, and we shall be alone."

Outside, Reverend Bayley's friends gather to shake his hand and clap him on the shoulder.

"It's time, Mistress Bayley. I'll swing ye onto the wagon and pass the children up."

I clutch my sister one last time.

"Ye'll always be in my heart," I whisper.

"And ye in mine," Mary replies. "And we shall write letters when we can."

Mary smooths an errant lock of hair off my face and turns to her husband, who boosts her onto the wagon. Reverend Bayley settles his family, tips his hat, and slaps the horses' reins. When he commands the two-horse team to walk on, the wagon lurches briefly until the horses find a steady pace.

My husband comes up behind me and puts his hands on my shoulders. "I know this is hard for ye," he says, "but it's Jehovah's will."

I nod, silently crying.

Tom picks up his daughter. "It's time for us to be away home."

Trudging behind my husband, my sorrow morphs into a premonition. What if my sister's departure wasn't Jehovah's doing but the devil's?

Thomas Putnam, the Younger

April 1682
Tom Putnam's House

I squint at the notice I received from the quarterly court before reading it for the third time.

"This can't be right," I mutter.

Ann comes in from outside with my daughter on her hip. The child smiles, reaching out her arms for me. "Papa!"

"Not now," I say, waving her away.

"Is that a letter?" Ann asks. "Who is it from?"

"The quarterly court. The magistrates ruled on yer father's estate."

Ann puts down our child, away from the fire, and joins me at the table. "What does it say?"

"Essentially, it says we've been robbed," I report furiously. "Yer father's estate is valued at eleven hundred pounds. Yer mother and yer brothers George and James will receive one hundred eighty pounds each."

"And what will the rest of us receive?"

"Ye and yer remaining five siblings each receive ninety pounds."

Ann's jaw drops. "That can't be right," she says, bewildered. "George should have the double portion, but James should have the same as the rest of us—though the extra ninety pounds won't make much of a difference."

"I shall not accept the court's ruling," I declare. "We deserve more. *Ye* deserve more. I shall contact the other heirs and petition the court."

"Are ye sure? My mother can be very clever."

"We shall ask for an independent appraisal, and the court will see they were misled." I begin trimming a pen. "I shall write the other family members immediately. I am determined we shall have yer fair inheritance."

Sarah Solart

November 1, 1682
Salem Common

From the corner of my eye, I glance at my escort. Daniel Poole isn't a handsome man. His hair is a bit long and his shoulders somewhat stooped. He is, however, the first man to pay me serious attention. If he holds my arm a little too snugly for propriety, he isn't obvious about it as we wander across the Common.

"Tell me, Goodwife Solart, though wife ye've yet to be, how is it a lass such as yerself lacks a husband?"

"I have no dowry," I say simply.

"I find myself astonished. Does yer family not provide for ye?"

"I have a roof over my head. Alas, my father departed to be with the angels ten years ago, and though I'm entitled to an inheritance, it remains elusive." I feel a twinge of shame. "And ye, sir," I say to change to subject, "is it true ye are part of Goodman Rowden's household?"

"That I am," he answers, smirking. "Which is why I'm a good catch for a young lady such as yerself. I've heard yer inheritance promises to be substantial. Am I correct?"

I sigh and resist the urge to turn on my heel and walk away. Another potential suitor who shall no doubt be disappointed by what I'm about to tell him and consider today, this time spent in my company, to be a waste.

May as well tell the truth and get it over with.

"I'm embarrassed to say it is unlikely I or my siblings shall ever see it. The courts ruled on our behalf, but . . . I remain an unmarried woman and am forced to dwell in my brother-in-law's household."

I stop walking and turn to face my escort.

"That being said, we should conclude our walk."

To my surprise, Daniel squeezes my hand. "Nay, lass. I have a better idea. We need to visit the shops. A new frock will do ye good. Something of quality."

"And how shall we pay for this? Have ye coin?"

He winks. "As John Rowden's sole heir, shopkeepers are happy to extend credit to me. Come."

I hesitate. The invitation is most inappropriate. I hardly know Goodman Poole, and thus it is improper to accept gifts from him.

"Goodwife Solart, ye disappoint me," he says. "May I not tempt ye with a new garment? Something made of canvas? Perhaps a petticoat to brighten yer dress? Allow me to escort ye to Captain Browne's shop. I need a new suit of clothes, and he's just got in a quantity of kersey wool."

"How do ye know?"

"My tailor told me. I need to select about seven yards and take it to him. It's no trouble to add canvas, and perhaps a printed fabric for the surface of yer petticoat?"

I shouldn't. "I suppose there's no harm in going into the shop with ye."

"Of course not, and if ye want to purchase something, ye've only to tell me."

Sarah Solart

Captain Browne's Shop

Captain Browne's shop has an outside entrance next to his warehouse. Inside, fine fabrics fill the shelves. My eyes strain to see the cloth more closely in the dim afternoon light that filters through the front window.

"Good morrow, Captain Browne," Daniel says.

The sea captain turns from appraising his stock and extends his hand in greeting. "Goodman Poole. It's good to see ye again. Ye must have heard of the fabrics I brought back from England. I've kersey wool, serge, canvas. Perhaps a few fripperies for yer companion?"

I step behind Daniel, hoping the captain doesn't recognize me as a barmaid at the ordinary, when Daniel grips my elbow and pulls me to his side. I sense my cheeks warming in embarrassment. *What must the captain think of me?*

"I should like to see the kersey wool ye have," Daniel declares. "I need a new suit of clothing. And my companion would like to see something suitable for . . . Forgive me, Goodwife Solart, I don't quite remember the garment ye mentioned."

I must stop this foolishness. "Thank ye, Goodman Poole, but I have no need of anything."

"Of course ye do. Yer clothing is very worn. Please allow me this one small favor."

I hesitate and drop my head. "Have ye anything suitable for a petticoat?"

Captain Browne gazes at me for a moment before he answers, as though I have broken the bounds of propriety. "We have canvas that will hold its shape, and also serge, which is quite nice."

A young boy enters the shop from the warehouse.

"Ah, Matthew will take care of yer purchase," Captain Browne says. "I have other matters to address. Matthew, show Goodman Poole the kersey, serge, and canvas. Maybe also add the printed fabric. Ye can add Goodman Poole's purchases to his invoice."

"Yes, Captain Browne." Matthew retrieves the fabrics from the shelves behind him. "Will ye take the kersey?"

"Yes, about seven yards, I should think. And the cost is . . . ?"

"Nine shillings for the yard."

"Yes, I'll have it. What about ye, Goodwife Solart?"

I run my hands over the canvas. It would make a strong petticoat, and then I could put the fabric with the printed design on top as the last petticoat. People would focus on the petticoats' affect and perhaps not notice the dull sheen on my dress.

But no, I cannot accept it, especially from a man I hardly know.

"It's lovely to see such fine fabric." I run my hand over the fabric's surface again and pinch it between my fingers. "No." I look out the window. "I cannot accept such a gift."

Daniel sighs. "Very well. Please add the petticoat fabrics to my order, and also nine yards of the serge."

"Ye shouldn't do that," I murmured. "The gossip will destroy me more than I already am."

"Gossip from whom?" Daniel scoffs. "Master Browne won't say anything, and who would listen to an apprentice?"

Behind us, the door opens.

"Is that ye, Goodman Poole? I've not seen ye for several weeks."

Daniel nods. "Goodwife Cody."

Goodwife Cody walks over to the counter. "And who is this with ye?" she asks, eyes leaping off my own until recognition dawns. "Ah, 'tis ye Goodwife Solart. How do ye do?"

Much to my chagrin, the woman glances between Daniel and I before noticing the items on the counter and surely piecing it all together. I can't even muster a response. My sense of guilt freezes me in place.

She knows Daniel is buying me fabric. She'll think . . .

I hang my head in shame when Daniel places the parcel of fabric under his arm and guides me to the door. The sound of Matthew's voice asking to serve Goodwife Cody follows me outside.

Sarah Solart

Two Weeks Later, November 1682
Joseph Lovett's House

"Sarah Solart and Daniel Poole, do the two of ye wish to wed?" the magistrate asks.

"We do," Daniel and I answer in unison.

"Excellent." The magistrate shakes Daniel's hand. "Goodman and Goodwife Poole, may yer marriage be long and fruitful."

My brother-in-law, Joseph Lovett, pours out five small glasses of Madeira. He passes one to the magistrate and to my sister Lizzie, his wife, before picking up his own. I accept a glass from my husband as my brother-in-law proposes a toast to us.

"To a long and happy life together. Welcome to the family, Goodman Poole."

"Thank ye." Daniel pulls me to his side. "My wife and I appreciate yer hospitality."

When my new husband winks at me, I feel slightly embarrassed. I still can't believe my good fortune. Daniel is Goodman Rowden's heir. He can have any young woman in Salem, yet he chooses me.

Yesterday, two weeks after acquiring the fabric and dropping it off with the tailor, Daniel had appeared at my brother-in-law's door with a parcel under his arm. I will never forget the sight of him. He smiled, revealing the dimple in his cheek.

"I have something for ye," he'd said. "Walk with me, and I'll give it to ye."

I'd grabbed my hat and walked outside. We walked in companionable silence until I could no longer contain my curiosity. "What is in the package, Goodman Poole?"

"Do ye remember our visit to Captain Browne's shop?"

"I shall never forget my embarrassment before Goodwife Cody," I'd said, certain the gossip was already spreading.

And yet Daniel appeared unaffected.

"Ye've nothing to be embarrassed about," he'd said. "My suit of clothes and yer petticoats, which I carry under my arm, are for a very special event."

"And what might that be?"

Daniel stopped walking and turned to face me. "Goodwife Solart, ye would make me a very happy man if ye would consent to marry me and wear the petticoats I had made for ye to wear at the ceremony."

My jaw had dropped.

"I needed a new suit for the occasion," he continued, "and I did not want ye to decline my offer because ye lacked suitable clothing for the event."

"Have ye planned everything?" I whispered.

"I have. I made arrangements with yer brother-in-law and the magistrate to have the ceremony at yer brother-in-law's house tomorrow afternoon. I only require yer agreement."

"What about the banns?"

"I paid for a special license."

My heart pounded. Blood rushed into my head. I almost fainted. "But I have no dowry," I had to remind him, certain that this was some kind of a mistake. Had he forgotten that I not only didn't have a dowry but also wasn't likely to receive an inheritance? What, precisely, did he have to gain from marrying me?

"I shall join yer siblings in a suit for yer proper inheritance," he explained. "Whatever we gain will be yer dowry."

"And if we gain nothing?"

"I shall have the best wife a man could have. Will ye accept my suit? Will ye marry me?"

I almost fainted while Daniel waited for my reply. "My answer is and always will be *yes*."

Daniel passed me the parcel of petticoats. "In that case, ye'd better have this."

I clutched the package to my chest in disbelief. After all I had lost, I now had a home and someone to love me.

"Sarah . . . Sarah?"

The memory in my head fades.

"What are ye thinking about?" my new husband asks.

"I was thinking about yesterday when ye asked me to marry ye."

"And not today when we are married?" he inquires with a sly smile.

"I am twenty-eight years old. I never expected to marry. But now, ye have chosen me, and I am a goodwife in truth."

"So shall ye always be." Daniel smooths a stray hair away from my face. "Come, it's time to go to yer new home."

Bursting with happiness, I place my hand on Daniel's arm. Such happiness may not be mine to keep, but I shall hold on to it as long as I can.

Sarah Solart Poole

April 1683
Daniel Poole's House

Venison stew with squash is tasty, but it's impossible to scoop all the residue out of the bowl with just bread. I clean and stack the bowls before putting them back into the cupboard. Thankfully, there's more stew left in the pot for tomorrow, so I only have to bake more bread.

Daniel touches my shoulder.

"Will ye come with me to check on the cow and her calf?" he asks. "I'm going to start selling the milk."

I give him a bewildered look. "What would I know about that?"

Daniel shrugs. "Have ye heard from yer brother-in-law Lovett?"

I purse my lips and shake my head. "Nay, but it's too soon. Court didn't come into session until last week."

"'Tis a simple case. Yer mother's husband stole yer inheritance."

"Spent it, more like," I agree. "The court ruled in our favor before, but nothing came of it. My share was only forty-two pounds when the magistrates ruled ten years ago, and I'm sure Master Woodward has spent most of that, never to be seen again."

I wipe my hands on my apron.

With a sigh, I say, "Let's see to the cow."

My husband and I link hands. In my husband's house, I feel secure—until Daniel brings up my inheritance, that is, which he does frequently. He has Master Rowden's patronage. Why does he need more? I push the thought aside and squeeze my husband's hand.

The black Kerry cow with her dark-tipped white horns grazes in the shady area of the pasture closest to our cottage while her calf noses her udder. I hold out my hand, offering the mother a bit of squash from dinner.

"See what I have for ye, Bess," I coo. Bess licks my hand with her rough tongue. "Ouch!"

Daniel laughs. "She gets ye every time. I tell ye to wear gloves, but ye dinna listen. Now yer hand's scratched."

I rub Bess's cheek. "No matter, darling. Ye don't mean to scratch me."

The calf detaches from Bess's udder and sniffs me.

"Ye dear creature, it's time to name ye. What do ye think, Daniel? Shall we call the calf Blackie?"

Daniel raises his eyebrows. "It's not very original, but it suits well enough."

"Master Poole!"

"Look! It's my brother-in-law," I say. "Perhaps he has news."

I motion for my brother-in-law to go into the house, wipe my hands on my apron, and follow Daniel through the gate.

"Goodman Lovett," Daniel says. "Come inside."

"Thankee, I will."

Sarah Solart Poole

Inside Daniel Poole's House

"How does my sister?" I ask my brother-in-law while pouring out small beer.

"Goodwife Lovett does well, as do our children."

"I am glad to hear it. Do ye—"

"What news have ye?" Daniel interrupts. "Have ye heard from the court?"

Goodman Lovett swallows his beer and belches. "Sister, I must tell ye that the court ruled in our favor, but . . ."

"Jehovah be praised!" Daniel interrupts again. "This is very good news."

"How so?" I ask. "A ruling is nothing without enforcement. We had a ruling ten years ago, for all the good it did us."

"If I may continue?" Goodman Lovett glances at Daniel, who nods. "My sister is correct, but without the ruling, we have nothing. As it stands, the court ruled Woodward deprived us, and the court will attach his house, land, cider press, and mill."

"When?" Daniel asks.

"When the writ is served, I suppose." Goodman Lovett stands and stretches. "I must be off home, and we must all be patient. Sister, Goodman Poole . . ." Goodman Lovett picks up his hat. "I bid ye farewell."

When the door closes, Daniel grins. "We did it, poppet. We'll build a proper house, and I can invest our profits. Perhaps we shall be merchants," he muses.

I don't express my doubts. With so many heirs, it's unlikely my father's legacy will be large enough to make much difference in our fortunes. But then again, I never expected to have that new petticoat.

Sarah Solart Poole

April 1683
Ye Burying Point, Salem Town

Shivering in the biting wind that blows in from the sea, I stare at the open gravesite.

Daniel's plain coffin lies in the pit, like a reproach on my life. The new year started so well. Daniel gave me the gift of an orange, though how he'd obtained it, I can't imagine. He'd said traders brought it from Madeira. I remember expecting the fruit to be sweet and juicy, but the taste was tart, as if to foretell the bitterness I now feel.

A week ago, Daniel came home with a chill. By the next morning, he had a high fever.

Two days later, he died.

I sigh and stare into the grave. My brother-in-law presses frozen soil into my hand. The others in attendance stand behind me, awaiting the completion of my final goodbye. And yet I can't seem to make it. Our lives had only just begun together.

"Ye must throw it into the grave," my brother-in-law murmurs. "And we must leave before we all catch a chill."

Sorrow fills my heart. "I don't want to throw dirt on my husband. I'd rather throw myself into his grave."

Joseph turns me to face him. "Such talk is a sin against Jehovah. Now, throw in the soil so the laborers can fill the grave, and we can all get warm."

"No. I can't."

Joseph aligns his arm and hand with mine and forces me to drop the clod of earth into my husband's grave before throwing in his own. He nods to the diggers, who begin shoving sodden soil into the burial pit.

Thomas Putnam, the Younger

April 1683
Sergeant Tom Putnam's House

How did this happen?

I rub the back of my neck, dislodging my hat. My fists curl in frustration. When I married Ann Carr, I had every right to expect a generous portion from her father's will—something to tide me over until my father died and I received my own inheritance.

My wife's father George Carr had been the richest man in Salisbury. He'd controlled the ferry across the Merrimack River connecting Amesbury with Newbury. He'd had livestock, cattle, and horses. Ann told me about growing up in a house where she wanted for nothing.

Before the Bayleys left Salem, I'd talked to my brother-in-law about reasonable expectations. His family lived in Newbury, and he was familiar with the Carr family. Reverend Bayley assured me it was as Ann said: her family was wealthy, and her father was fair.

Her father, however, had failed to make a will. How could he have been so irresponsible? Even as he knew his life was ending, he refused to make his wishes known. As such, it was left to the Essex quarterly court to rule on his property, and they knew nothing about it.

Their first disposition was unacceptable. After Ann's mother received her widow's portion and the court granted a double portion for James Carr in addition to the portion for George, the oldest son, there was little to divide. The appraisers valued the entire property at eleven hundred pounds, and my wife Ann received ninety pounds in a mixture with little actual money, a bit of livestock, and land. How can I use land in another county? I'll have the expense of selling it or renting it.

Don't worry, James Bayley had told me. *We'll appeal the ruling, have the property reappraised by honest men.* The matter went to the General Court and back to the quarterly court. Each time with fees to the court. James Bayley assured me the process would be worth it; our shares would increase.

I reach into my pocket to retrieve the court document that arrived at Ingersoll's Ordinary this morning. I read the document again and put it back into my pocket. James was as wrong as he was right. The ruling changed but not enough to matter. Ann's oldest brother got a double share. Her mother received her dower rights. James received a single portion with the rest of his siblings. Ann received a value of one hundred sixty pounds. But it wasn't money. Once again, it was mostly livestock and land of varying quality.

And now it is time to inform my wife.

The small inheritance won't bother her as much as her father's lack of consideration and planning, and her mother's apparent disinterest.

I knock the muck off my boots before entering the house. Inside, little Ann runs through the house, pulling her brother's carved wooden horse behind her. Young Thomas watches with tears of frustration running down his face. At the moment, I'm not interested in consoling my children.

"Ann," I scold. "Give yer brother back his toy."

"I'm playing with it," she says, pouting.

"Not anymore." I pick up the wooden horse and give it to Thomas before setting the toddler on his feet. Cautiously, the boy keeps one eye on his sister and begins pulling the horse behind him.

"Papa, I had it first."

"Perhaps ye did. But ye are the oldest and charged with looking after yer brother. Reducing him to tears is not acceptable. Do ye understand?"

Ann nods but clearly resents my discipline.

"What's going on?" Ann waddles into the room, heavily pregnant again.

"Yer daughter was tormenting our son. I've put a stop to it," I tell her. "Ye must keep a closer eye on them."

"I try. Perhaps we could buy papers for an indentured nursemaid. I expect our newcomer to arrive next month, and I can't care for so many children as well as the house and garden by myself."

"Ye need to sit down. I have something else to discuss." I walk my wife to a wooden stool by the table, where she sits. "The court at Ipswich issued its ruling on yer father's estate."

Ann's eyes light up. "Did they rule fairly this time?"

"I'm sure they think they did, under the circumstances. Yer mother and brothers did not cooperate with the committee."

"I'm sure they did not. They don't wish to make a fair accounting. So what did the court rule?"

"Yer mother receives her dower portion, plus eighty-seven pounds' worth of stock or movables. Yer brother, George, as the eldest son, receives three hundred twenty pounds."

"And the rest of us?"

"Yer other brothers, ye, and yer sisters each receive one hundred sixty pounds from the estate. I'm sure I needn't tell ye that I'm disappointed in the outcome, especially after the expense of contesting the first distribution."

Ann's eyes fall to her large belly. She swallows several times and shakes her head. "So our fortunes have not improved?"

"Not as much as I hoped."

She nods and raises her eyes to meet mine—and though I can tell she's disappointed, I sense she is more disappointed that *I'm* disappointed. "I suppose we shall have to make the best of it."

"I hear some indentured servants just arrived from Jersey," I tell her, sighing. I offer her a warm smile. "We may have enough to purchase papers for one of them."

Ann gives me a wavering smile in return. "That would be a blessing. Mind ye hire an industrious girl."

I kiss Ann's forehead, glad to see hope return to her eyes.

Sarah Solart Poole

Two Weeks Later
Daniel Poole's House

I drop the last coin into my small pouch. The purse feels heavy, but I know it's a trick.

For the third time, I pour the silver coins out and begin counting them again. I lift each coin between my fingers to eye level so I can examine it. This one with the pine tree in the middle is worth a pound and has the numerals *XII* on the back. I got it when I sold the horse.

I put the coin aside and look at each of my other coins, separating them. Some have an oak tree with two bushes. Others have a willow tree. On the reverse side are numbers: *III* or *VI*. I separate out the *VIs* from the *IIIs* and count on my fingers.

Two VIs *is one pound. I have six of these for one entire cow and half of the other.*

I stop to remember Bess and her calf Blackie. *They were sweet animals. I hope they like their new home.*

For the other cow, I have the half in shillings and the rest in pence. *Two pence, four pence . . .*

I stop when I reach one hundred twenty pence.

I don't have enough. It looks like a lot of money, but it's not.

I wring my hands in fear and pull my hair, dislodging my coif in the process. *What can I do? I can't pay for Daniel's coffin. I'll die in debtor's prison!* I reach for the coins and scoop them off the table and back into my purse. Then I put my purse into the pocketbook inside my dress.

The only thing I can do is sell something more.

I look around the room, as though something valuable will jump out at me. The cart will be here soon to take the furniture. I can go to my sister's house, but I can't stay there long. Lizzie was adamant about that. *She didn't have to be so mean about it. Maybe I can work in an ordinary—*

I hear footsteps outside, then a light knock on the door.

I hold my head in my hands and ignore the door.

"Goodwife Poole," a voice calls. "May I come in?"

I look up to see a well-dressed man standing in the doorway. I pat the pocketbook beneath my dress.

"Are ye here for the furniture?" I ask.

"No." The man takes off his hat and sits by me at the table. "My name is John Cromwell. I am a merchant, of sorts. I understand ye are selling up."

"Ye're too late. Everything is sold," I tell him, failing to conceal my misery. "The last of our belongings will be picked up today, and then I will have nothing."

I pull my hand over my face, too tired to listen to this stranger.

"Perhaps I can help," Cromwell says. "As an act of charity, I am willing to pay yer outstanding debts and yer husband's funeral costs."

I drop my hands, blinking back at him. "Why would ye do that? I canna pay ye back."

"Perhaps ye can. I'm told yer family is petitioning the quarterly court for yer father's inheritance."

"We won't prevail."

"On the chance that ye might," he wagers, "I am willing to defray yer debts. If ye receive any recompense, ye can pay me back. If ye don't, I'll have done an act of charity both for ye and for yer creditors."

I look closely at this Master Cromwell. His suit is the finest kersey wool. His cravat looks like it is made of silk. *If he's telling the truth, he can pay my debts and never miss the coin.*

"What do ye want from me?" I ask him.

"Nothing. When ye come into yer inheritance, I shall sue ye in the courts for the debt."

Outside, a wagon pulls up.

"They're here to collect the furniture."

"Do we have an agreement?" Cromwell asks.

I take a deep breath. *I've lost everything already. What harm can it do?*

"Hallo?" Two laborers stand in the doorway in their work boots and heavy coats.

Cromwell rises and offers his hand.

"Goodwife Poole?"

"Yes. I agree."

"I shall pay yer debts this week. Good day."

Such a strange sensation. A man in fine clothing leaving my home. Rough workmen coming in to take the last of my belongings. Daniel gone to the angels. My life a tapestry of broken dreams.

I wrap myself in my wool cloak, hunch my shoulders to keep in the warmth, and begin walking to my sister Lizzie's house.

What shall become of me? Anything? Nothing?

Sarah Solart Poole

February 1686
A shed in Salem Village

My head jerks up from the straw where I fell asleep. I'm in some sort of shed.

I hear the distinct *bawk-bawk-bawk-bawkah!* of a chicken's egg song and realize at once that I'm not just in a shed, I'm in a *coop*. I place my hands flat onto the straw and push myself into a sitting position. Chinks in the wall admit weak light into the shed. I look around.

A chicken flies out from the far corner.

Yes! That hen definitely laid an egg. I just have to steal it.

I keep an eye on the chicken scratching the straw on the other side of the coop and quietly shuffle toward the corner. Outside, a rooster crows, drawing the hen's attention. I find a nest with three eggs in it. My mouth waters as I snatch them and put them into my pocket to eat later.

A skinny boy swings the shed door open from the outside. "Ye! Wot ye doin' here? Begone wid ye! We don't harbor villains."

"I done no harm," I whine. "Just slept outta da cold. I'm goin'."

I drop my head and pass the youth on my way out the door. Away from the house, I stop in a meadow and pull out my eggs. One is cracked but still has half its yolk. I lick out the shell, savoring the texture. Then I crack each of the remaining eggs and slurp the contents out of their shells.

I check my pocket again in case I have another egg. *It's so hard to remember.* The pocket is empty, so I resume my search for Daniel. *We only just married. Why did he leave me?*

William Good

February 1686
Ingersoll's Ordinary, Salem Village

The roaring fire in the great room is a welcome respite from the brisk February air. The sun promises spring, but the whipping wind denies it and forces everybody back indoors.

I look at the breakfast offerings, feel the coins in my pocket, and walk to the bar.

"What'll ye have?" the innkeeper's wife asks.

"A tankard of ale and porridge," I decide, going with the least expensive options.

I put my money on the bar, pick up my tankard of ale, and stop by the food table to ladle the coagulated oats masquerading as porridge into an old, scratched wooden bowl.

"Billy Boy—over here!" I hear somebody say.

I glance over my shoulder and smile. I wouldn't call Eben a good friend, but he has proven to be a useful acquaintance. I've gotten work from him over the last few years, and I daresay, I would not disagree to more work now, considering the lack of weight in my pocket.

I walk over to a table near the fire. After setting my food down, I grasp hands with a slightly older man who established himself by marrying a prosperous widow. From time to time, he hires me to do odd jobs. I straighten my back, so he'll think I'm fit. "Eben," I say. "Good to see ye. Ye need help with the farm? Fencing or—"

"Ye lookin' fer work?" Eben asks.

"Aye. Figure people want to start gardens or prepare fields, or mebbe ye need to rebuild yer walls."

"I might have somethin'—but listen, son," he says, giving me a pointed look. "Ye ever think of settlin' down?"

I laugh. "I've no money for a wife."

"What if a wife had money for *ye*? Would ye marry?"

Again, I laugh. "Mebbe. Ye have someone in mind?"

"As it happens. If I was unmarried, I'd take advantage, but my wife is very much alive. So, if I share information, and ye succeed, would ye remember who helped ye?"

"I doubt ye'd let me forget."

"True enough. Are ye interested?"

"Mebbe."

Eben pauses to drink some ale while I wipe out my porridge bowl with bread. It's a bit out of character, this pause of his. He's thinkin' over his words carefully. "Do ye remember old man Solart in Wenham?"

"Never been to Wenham," I say.

"He died about ten years ago, an' the family's been fighting for their inheritance ever since."

"What's that ta do wid me?"

"One of the heirs is Daniel Poole's derelict widow. They weren't married a month before he took ill and died. Lass hasn't been in 'er right head since."

"Still don't see a connection, and I need to get on." I start to leave.

Eben motions me back down. "Here's the thing," he whispers. "The inheritance went through. Marry the woman, and it's yers." He leans back. "What do ye think of that?"

"Ye can't be serious. Marry a widow who's out of her head so I can get her inheritance? Do ye know how much it is?"

"More than ye have now. I heard she got a meadow."

"In Wenham?"

"Ye can rent it or sell it. Ye'd still be better off than ye are now."

I stroke my chin. "Where do I find this woman?"

"Widow Poole? She wanders around. Look in the open spaces. Ye'll find 'er."

William Good

Salem Village

I spend most of the day looking for this widow, but it isn't until twilight that I spot a ragged woman with her hat askew and her clothing hanging off her body who is . . . well, quite visibly *out of her head*, as Eben put it.

Must be her.

When I get closer to her, I see she doesn't wear a coif, and her gray hair flies around her face.

"Hallo!" I call in my most cheerful voice, waving my hand in greeting. The woman looks in my direction and clutches a bundle to her side, staring back at me as though I'm the mad one.

"Ye shan't have this," she says. "It's mine!"

"I mean ye no harm," I say, holding out my hands in a calming motion. The woman grunts and pulls her bundle closer. I slowly approach her and smile. "Ye must be cold. Come wid me. We'll find a fire."

The woman's eyes look past me before returning to my face.

"Who are ye?" she asks.

"A friend to help ye. Are ye Widow Poole?"

"They call me that—but my husband's coming back," she says with certainty, a wildness to her eyes that is off putting and sad in equal measure. "He is!" she snaps, sensing my skepticism. "I'm sure of it. When I remember where he went, I can bring him home."

"Nay, lass," I say softly. "Yer husband be wid the angels."

Tears slide down the woman's face. There's a moment of dire silence. I can practically see the comprehension dawn on her face, the grief still fresh. "Yes . . . Yes, I . . . I remember now," she says softly. "The gravesite was just off the ocean."

I put my arm around the woman's shoulders and guide her back toward the ordinary. Every step of the way, she sobs.

"May I call ye Sarah?" I ask. "And ye must call me William, or Bill."

"William," she whispers. "That's a nice name. My husband had a nice name. He saved me. I was nothing, and he married me. But . . . then he died."

"He did," I agree. "But we're together now. It will be like before. I'll take care of ye. Come inside."

At the bar, I order stew, ale, and a room upstairs with a bath before escorting Sarah to a small table near the fire. Men pull their chairs away when we pass. I can't blame them. The woman is filthy and smells like the privy. She eats with desperation, using her hands and watching me as if I'll snatch her food away. Her eyes shift around the room. Her leg bounces up and down, shaking the table.

Watching her strange behavior, I wonder if I have the courage to marry her. She's been living rough too long to be a fit wife. But with secure housing and a regular diet, she might rally. And there's the meadow to consider. Yes, I decide to risk it, even if she turns out to be a shrew.

William Good

April 1686
Salem Village

I neatly stack four armloads of split logs by the hearth before I stand and dust off my hands on my trousers. "That should keep us for a bit. Wid it bein' spring, we only need the fire for cooking. Stew pot smells pretty good."

I smile with satisfaction. We've only been married for two months, and Sarah has turned out to be a far better wife than I'd ever expected. Her cooking is adequate for my tastes, and she keeps my bed warm.

"I put pork fat in the porridge."

"But no pork?" I ask.

"We've no coin for that." Sarah looks at me with dull eyes. "We can't pay for this cottage."

I sit down next to my wife on a bench near the fire and turn to face her.

"Goody Good, ye are my wife, are ye not?"

Sarah nods. "Aye."

"And ye inherited a meadow from yer father. Do ye remember?"

"I did?"

"Yes. Last month, ye and yer sisters inherited yer father's estate, and we received Thorndike's Meadow near Wenham, where ye grew up."

"A meadow. Is it large?"

"Mebbe five acres. We rent it to local farmers, so we'll have coin soon." I give her an especially sly grin. "Enough to put actual *pork* in the porridge."

I kiss my wife's forehead.

"So we've nothing to worry about. I'm off to the ordinary, but I'll be back for our dinner."

I whistle as I walk along the road to the village. I'll have a couple tankards of ale and then go home for my meal. Turns out Eben was right. I have an unusual wife, but I also have plenty of coin.

William Good

Ingersoll's Ordinary, Salem Village

Entering the ordinary, I hang my outer coat on a peg by the door and cross to the bar.

"Goodman Good," the barman says. "Tankard of ale?"

"Please, and put it on my account. I'll settle when the income from our new meadow comes through."

The barman slides me a tankard of ale. "There's a gentleman lookin' for ye."

"What fer?"

"He didn't say. That's him over there," he says, nodding to across the way. "Near the window."

I pick up my tankard and walk over to the man's table. "Barman says ye're lookin' for me."

The man glances up, and I take his measure. Clearly, the stranger is prosperous. His clothing is tailored, and his food . . . I inhale the smell of beef stew. I can see the chunks of meat in the stranger's bowl. The porridge with pork fat waiting for me at home is swill by comparison.

"Are ye perchance Goodman Good?" he asks.

"I am, and who might ye be?"

"Henry Skerry, marshal for the Essex County quarterly court. Allow me to finish my meal, and I shall explain further."

I sip my ale and watch Skerry chew. I think he may be missing a few teeth. After about twenty minutes, Skerry wipes out his bowl with bread and finishes his meal.

The barman appears at Skerry's elbow. "Anythin' else?"

"Aye. Bring me a tankard of ale."

The barman picks up the bowl and scurries away. Skerry reaches into his pocket and pulls out some documents, and I presume he's ready to get down to business. "According to these, ye recently came into yer wife's inheritance of a five-acre meadow called Thorndike's Meadow."

My belly lurches; I start sweating. "Aye."

"Did ye know yer wife owes a sizable debt to John Cromwell?"

"No."

"Ah, well . . ." He scoffs, tapping the paperwork. "Let me enlighten ye . . ."

"Debt, ye say?"

"Yes." Skerry looks through the documents again. "Master Cromwell paid several debts yer wife accrued during her marriage to Daniel Poole. He sued at this quarter's court at Ipswich for the funds, which came to seven pounds, eight shillings, and nine pence—to be paid in corn or cattle. In addition, court costs are nine pence, and my services to execute the court order are two shillings."

"But, sir," I say, very much regretting coming here, "we only received the meadow last month. We've yet to receive any rental fees."

"Alas, such matters are in Jehovah's hands." Skerry hands me a document. "The magistrates authorized me to seize three acres of meadow to compensate Master Cromwell for his debt. There's still a bit of the meadow left for yer use—almost two acres, I believe."

He rises from the table, leaving me astonished.

"Allow me to pay for yer ale on my way out. Contact the court if ye have questions."

"Yes, sir," I mumble, unable to get myself to move from this spot. *I arrived here with a five-acre meadow and expectations of a solid income and pork in my porridge. Now, I have less than two acres, and a barmy wife.*

Thomas Putnam, the Younger

May 18, 1686
Lieutenant Thomas Putnam's Funeral

Like almost everyone present for the funeral, I indulged in too much rum punch last night while listening to everyone's memories of what a fine man my father was. *Lieutenant Thomas Putnam. Yeoman farmer. Militia officer. Quarterly court constable. Parish clerk. Wealthiest man in Salem Village.* I slapped backs, joined in the stories about my father, and drank.

Now, mourners take their places behind the coffin.

My brothers and I drape the black broadcloth pall over Father's coffin, hiding the underbearers beneath it. As the eldest son, I take the leading position and hold the pall's fabric corner at the left forward position. My brother Edward should be on my right, but my half-brother Joseph stands there instead. Brother Edward and my deceased sister Anne's husband William Trask hold the back two corners. Behind them, my stepmother, escorted by our minister Deodat Lawson, leads other family relations and prominent members of Salem Village on the short pathway from my father's house to the Putnam Burying Ground.

As we walk, I nod to acknowledge the many townspeople standing to pay their respects from the side of the road. Aside from occasional squawks from seabirds and the sound of the village bell, the procession passes in absolute silence.

At the gravesite, the underbearers reveal themselves. Together, with the family pallbearers, each grabs an end of the ropes positioned under the coffin and lowers their burden into the empty grave pit before withdrawing the ropes. In silence, everyone picks up soil to throw over the coffin before the gravediggers close the site.

When the others withdraw to return to the house, Ann joins my side and clasps my hand, entwining our fingers.

"'Tis a sad day," she says. "I remember when my sister and I arrived with Reverend Bayley, how yer father welcomed us into his home. He was a generous man."

"Aye."

"Shall we return? Food and drink will be set out, and people expect to see ye."

I draw my lips into a line. "It seems like we've been feeding the town for the past week."

"It isn't every day a man like yer father goes to the angels. Come, ye cannot evade yer obligations."

I draw a deep breath, exhale, and turn back to the path.

Thomas Putnam, the Younger

July 1686
Ingersoll's Ordinary

Sitting at a table near the back of Ingersoll's Ordinary, I watch patrons enter to buy food and drink for their midday meal. Soon it will be time to drill the militia on the village common area. I wonder if now that my father is with the angels, I'll be promoted to lieutenant.

I toss back my glass of rum, relishing the burn at the back of my throat and the way it soothes the dull ache in my chest. I grieve not just the loss of my father but his unforeseen betrayal. Soon, everyone in Salem Village will know that the court ruled against my efforts to overturn Father's will. Brother Joseph will no doubt chortle as he shares the news. I motion to the serving lad to bring me another round.

The man I'd idolized all my life turned his back on his eldest son, leaving the best of everything to his youngest. *Leave him coin and cattle, if ye must, but not the family homestead and the best farmland.* When the lad puts down my next glass, I hand him some coins before taking a long drink of the sharp, golden liquid.

Unsettled thoughts enter my rum-fueled haze. *Father favored me until my stepmother gave him a son, who became the apple of his eye. How could a man overlook his firstborn? Yet he did. The woman and her son whispered in his ear and took what was mine.*

I slam my glass down on the table, drawing a few glances from men beginning to gather for the afternoon drill.

"Don't stand there gawking!" I yell. "Form yerselves on the field!"

Exiting the ordinary, I hear men shuffling out behind me. I wait on the field until the men form their lines and then begin shouting orders for them to execute the drill.

"This isn't over," I vow to myself. "I will have my place as the leader of Salem Village."

William Good

Early Evening, August 1686
William Good's House

When I left the house this morning, Sarah stood at the hearth, stirring our stew pot. There was nothing in it but water and a few turnips. Six hours later, I return home to find my wife stirring the same pot. Judging by the complete lack of cooking aromas, I'm pretty sure my wife forgot to add anything to the pot. In fact, she may be stirring an empty cauldron, for all I know.

When the court confiscated three acres of my wife's meadow to pay the bills her first husband left, the loss of potential income destroyed my plans for an easy life. I went back to my previous occupation and did jobs for local farmers. But I'm not as agile as I once was, and farmers only hire me to fix fences or mow meadows in the hot sun.

It certainly doesn't help that Sarah isn't pleasant to be around. Quite the opposite, what with her stirring empty stew pots and looking for lost things she never finds. Today, Jehovah blessed my patience and generosity. The man who purchased a portion of Sarah's meadow from Cromwell wants the rest of it. He's offering five pounds for her two acres—in *silver*. My palm itches to feel the coin. *Five pounds!*

I take a chair by the table and call on my powers of persuasion. Busy stirring her pot, Sarah pays me no mind.

"Sarah, poppet, cease yer cooking and come sit with me. I have good news."

Sarah looks over her shoulder. "Not done yet. Needs a stir."

"Ye can stir in a minute. Come sit."

"Just a bit more," she mutters.

I rise and place my arm around Sarah's shoulders so I can walk her to the second chair by the table. She looks at me with a startled expression.

"Mustn't stop," she says. "'Twill burn."

"It can wait a bit."

I kneel next to my wife and stroke her back. "Sarah, can ye look at me? I have good news. A man wants to buy the rest of yer meadow at Wenham."

"Wenham?"

"Yes, poppet. Ye inherited a meadow there. Do ye remember?"

"I think so, but someone took it away. I don't 'member why. Do ye?"

"We lost part of the meadow because we had to pay yer debts. Do ye remember that?"

Sarah's eyes shift back over to the hearth. She starts to stand, still itching to get back to that empty pot and stir the air inside it.

I reach for her arm, grasping it softly. "No, Sarah. Sit. Focus on my words. We dinna lose the entire meadow, just enough to pay yer debts. But now, the man who owns the part we lost wants to buy the rest of it. He wants to give us five pounds. Isn't that a blessing?"

"Aye." Sarah nods. "And then we'll have enough coin?"

"Yes, poppet, we will." I hold Sarah's hands. "When ye sign a court document, we'll get five pounds in silver in exchange for that land."

I withdraw the document from my jacket and spread it on the table. Then I open the box where we have a dull quill pen and an inkwell. Sarah watches me dip the pen into the ink. I wrap her fingers near the nib and show her where to write her name.

"The ink is on the nib. Just write yer name here." I point to the bottom of the document and hold her hand above the spot. A small drop of ink lands on the parchment.

"Just put yer name here." I point again.

"Why?"

"Ye have dower rights in the meadow, and ye have to give them up, or else we won't get the five pounds."

Sarah holds the quill and seems to think about what I said. Another drop of ink falls.

"But then," she says, "I won't have anything."

I'm impatient but keep my voice low. "We won't have the meadow, but we'll have five pounds, which we very much need. Just sign yer name."

"I don't want to sign." She pouts. "I want the meadow. Father gave it to me. It's *mine*."

"Sarah . . ." I'm so frustrated I nearly take the pen and sign on her behalf. Except I can't write. Like most people, I can only read the Bible. "Sarah, poppet, we need the money, so please sign. Ye don't need dower rights. Ye have me."

I dip the pen nib again and hand the quill back to Sarah.

"Just put yer name here. Shall I help ye?" I ask, because I know she never wants help from me.

"No," she says. "I can do it."

She leans over the document and presses the pen nib into the parchment. Ink splashes with every scratch of her name: *S-A-R-A-H*. The mismatched letters glitter from the wet ink. *Will the court accept only one name? I don't think so.*

"Ye didn't finish, poppet. Ye need to write 'Good' next to 'Sarah.' Can ye do that?"

Sarah picks up the quill again and places the nib near the first word. She scratches the letters *G-O-O-D* onto the document. The ink is light, but it will have to do. I scatter sand over the wet ink to set it in place.

"No more meadow," Sarah says in a sing-song voice.

"No," I confirm. "No more meadow, but we have five pounds. Isn't that marvelous?"

Sarah pats my cheek. "Are ye happy with me?"

I squeeze her fingers. "Ye're a good wife."

I tuck the document back under my coat so I can send it to the court tomorrow. I wonder how long it will take to receive the five pounds.

Reverend Samuel Parris

November 25, 1688
Salem Village Meetinghouse

I raise my open hands to give the final blessing at the end of the worship service. By reputation, the people in the Salem Village church are a fractious lot. Since their congregation formed, three ministers have filled their pulpit. None held office long enough to be ordained. And now, Jehovah calls me to preach. *Will they invite me to take the pulpit on a permanent basis? If they do, should I accept? Where does Jehovah want me?*

I stop my wandering thoughts and intone the traditional prayer from the Book of Numbers. "The Lord bless thee and keep thee. The Lord make His face to shine upon thee and be gracious unto thee. The Lord lift up His countenance upon thee and give thee peace. Amen."

I dismiss the congregation, but interestingly, no one leaves their seats.

Deacon Ingersoll motions for me to step down from the pulpit and take a seat in the first row of benches.

"Thank ye for speaking to us this day," he says. "Please remain seated while we vote with a show of hands for ye to become our minister in our time of need."

My heart pounds in surprise. I didn't think the villagers were ready to fill the vacancy or that today would be the day they'd vote on it—with me present, no less. Jehovah's timing always feels right, but this feels *rushed*.

Deacon Ingersoll turns to those in attendance and says, "Those who support the proposition that we invite Reverend Samuel Parris to be our new minister at Salem Village, please raise yer right hand."

I turn in my seat and am surprised to see the majority of voting members raise their hands. Clearly, they want me to accept the pulpit, but there's no need to rush the process. Jehovah has a purpose for me, whether it is here or elsewhere.

"Reverend Parris, may we extend the offer of our pulpit to ye? Will ye join our village?"

Deacon Ingersoll looks confident that I will accept the pulpit, but I am suspicious. How can they discern Jehovah's will so quickly? Perhaps they think I am desperate enough to accept whatever conditions they offer.

"Ye do me great honor," I reply, "but such a decision is a weighty matter."

Deacon Ingersoll's face shifts from confidence to an expression of shock—and then to something that resonates as artificial neutrality. "Do ye decline our invitation?"

"On the contrary, I am humbled by yer offer," I say, getting to my feet and preparing to take my leave. "But I need to pray and discern Jehovah's will. Ye shall have yer answer in due course."

William Good

Spring 1689
Beverly, On the road to Gage Farm

Sarah clutches our daughter, Dorothy, on her hip.

"I kin take 'er," I say, reaching for the child—but Sarah recoils the same way she had the day I'd found her roaming the streets.

"No." Her eyes dart back and forth at our surroundings. "She's mine."

"Aye, but ye must be tired. Let me hold 'er for ye."

"Ye'll steal her away," she says, and I try not to sigh. My wife's madness is tiring. Dorothy cries and rubs her eyes. "Ye upset her now. Ye'll be fine, bairn . . . Mam has ye."

"Mayhap she be hungry," I say. "There's trees over there. We kin rest a bit. Come."

I leave the road and head toward a small copse of trees. *If Sarah sits, mayhap she'll let the child go.*

My wife perches on an overturned tree limb with Dorothy on her lap. "I've nothing for 'er." She turns toward me with a venomous stare. "It's yer fault. Ye canna keep a job nor shelter for us." She gazes at our child. "Yer pap will kill us both. What kin we do?"

I feel myself bristle, though I know better than to react. It never helps. Instead, I do what I have taken to doing more often than not: waiting for her attention to wane, to target something else, and for her to ultimately lose focus.

In perhaps a minute, my wife's eyes become blank, staring emptily into the distance.

As planned, I lift Dorothy into my arms and pat her back. "Come to yer pa." *Poor bairn. She's nothing but skin and bone.*

When Sarah's focus returns, she reaches her arms toward Dorothy.

"I have her, Sarah," I say. "Come. Walk with me, like a proper family."

We return to the road. I keep my eye out for a farm where we might find charity. I narrow my eyes on a likely destination.

"Sarah, do ye see the house up ahead?"

"Give 'er back," she whines.

"I will when we get to the house. The Gages live there. They have young ones so ye can gain their trust. We'll go ta door. Ye in front with Dorothy. I'll stay behind. Throw yerself on their sympathy. Do ye ken?"

Sarah nods. "Aye. Beg fer help. For Dorothy."

"Aye."

The yard around the house looks deserted in the sun's waning rays. At the doorway, I pass Dorothy to Sarah, knock, and withdraw to stand behind my family. A woman answers, holding a child's hand in each of hers. She looks Sarah up and down.

"Sarah, Mary, go inside the house. *Now.*" The woman turns her attention back to Sarah. "I've no time for beggars. Go ta town."

The woman starts to close the door.

Will Sarah hold it together?

"No! Please!" Sarah wheedles. "We come for Christian charity. My husband ain't got no work, and we're cast on the road. And my child . . . my little Dorothy." Sarah turns so the woman can see Dorothy's face. "See how thin she is? I canna feed her, and she'll die. Please!"

Sarah reaches out her hands, pushing toward the woman.

"Stay away!" the woman shouts. "Ye be filthy and bring the smallpox. Get away before ye make us sick!"

"No, no. We're not sick. Just tired an' hungry. Please help us. Jehovah says ye must." Sarah lifts Dorothy forward again. "Dinna turn yer back on us."

"Begone with ye!"

The woman turns away and slams the door.

"How dare she?" Sarah mumbles as we turn back toward the road. There's a darkness in her eyes that's more malignant than her typical temper.

I approach to soothe her, but it's no use, as she's now focused on the cattle surrounding the farm. "She be no Christian! Look at their cows!"

I do.

They are plenty, which is why I'd chosen this home for us to approach.

Sarah bares her teeth. "I curse them to fall down and die!" she says, so wickedly that it sends a chill up my spine. "I beg Jehovah to smite them all!"

Reverend Samuel Parris

April 1689
Salem Village Parsonage

The church committee members sit in the front room of the parsonage, paying me another call. For six months, I have lived in the parsonage while I preached to their small congregation. For six months, the church committee invited me to accept the pulpit in Salem Village.

But what should be a lifetime appointment seems unlikely to last that long. Members of the church are a minority in the village. I'll have to infuse them with spiritual commitment, and I don't know if they can make the transition. Nevertheless, I must try.

Deacon Ingersoll clears his throat. He sits beside the hearth, facing me. The position casts him in a silhouette, framing him in low flames. "Have ye had sufficient time to consider our pecuniary offer?"

"I have," I say, "and ye have my response: a salary of sixty pounds with use of the parsonage is a generous offer, but ye say that only twenty pounds will be paid in coin. The rest will be paid in so-called *country cash*. This gives me pause."

The men nod.

"Gentlemen, in such a situation, I must be notified in advance what people propose to pay me. I have no use, for example, for a calf's head or a swarm of bees, though grain, beef, and butter are useful items. Also, no mention is made of firewood. How, pray tell, am I to warm my house without firewood? I insist that wood be provided."

Deacon Ingersoll spreads his hands. "I speak for all of us when I say that providing wood is impossible, because we have no common woodland from which to harvest it. We can, however, add another six pounds to yer salary with two pounds of it in coin, so that ye may purchase thirty cords of wood at four shillings a cord, regardless of the current price."

"And which one of ye will guarantee the wood for purchase?"

The room falls silent.

I sigh and let the moment pass. Such matters can be discussed again later. I stand and hold out my hand. "Gentlemen, with Jehovah's guidance, I accept yer offer to serve Salem Village from the pulpit of yer church."

Thomas Putnam, the Younger

November 19, 1689
Salem Village Meetinghouse

Reverend Parris enters the church from the side door to greet the visiting clergy: Reverend Phillips from Rowley, Reverend Hale from Beverly, and Reverend Noyes from Salem Town. All sound men. Men whose support raises the status of the Salem Village church to one equal to any church in Boston. Of that I am certain.

The new minister moves with an air of confidence, as if he knows he has Jehovah's favor. More than that, he is a handsome man with his dark, shoulder-length hair, straight nose, and strong chin. He knows what he's about. The dissenters will not fool him, nor will he shy away from conflict.

I should greet the learned men, but I linger at the entry door instead. If Father were here, he would be among them, declaring the order of service. But these men don't need deacons to show them the way. Reverend Parris, in particular, knows Jehovah's ways and our role in the struggle between angels and demons.

Visitors from surrounding communities flow through our meetinghouse doors, filling the seats and standing at the sides of the room.

"Master Putnam, shall ye not take yer place?"

I look up to see my wife Ann shepherding our five children into the church.

"Yes." I hold out my arm. "I shall escort ye."

Together, we make our way to the front seating. I place my family directly behind Reverend Parris's wife and children. The women nod to each other before Ann settles our brood. I continue forward to the circle of ministers.

"Gentlemen," I say, "is it not time to begin the service?"

"Are ye prepared, Reverend Parris?" Reverend Noyes asks.

"I am."

"Very well, let us take our places."

I take my seat at the deacon's table, leaving the clergy to sit near the pulpit. Reverends Hale and Philips each offer an opening prayer beseeching Jehovah for grace and the ability to comprehend his mercy on our sins.

I bow my head. I often think Jehovah is punishing me, though I can't think of any reason for it. My brother has the inheritance that should have been mine. My wife's father denied Ann her proper legacy. And the nightmares about events from twenty years ago torture me every night.

How did I anger Jehovah?

I shake my head to clear it. Reverend Philips introduces Reverend Samuel Parris. The man confidently ascends into the pulpit, raises his hands in prayer, and begins preaching. I turn over the hourglass and place it where Reverend Parris can watch the time pass.

"My message this day is from the ninth verse in Joshua, chapter five: 'And the Lord said unto Joshua, this day have I rolled away the reproach of Egypt from ye.' In this," Parris continues, "Jehovah gave us a divine promise of faith. He kept his promise to give Canaan to Abraham, but only after he warned the Canaanites that, because of their idolatry, he would root them out of the earth and give their land to a better people."

I turn the hourglass and consider Reverend Parris's admonition. Many of those present for the ordination service are not members of our church and oppose Reverend Parris's appointment, yet they came to watch. *What are they plotting?*

Reverend Parris continues his remarks, saying that everyone must meet Jehovah in the work of this day and enter the covenant of grace.

"I," Reverend Parris says, "will carry my work as the Lord's servant. I shall make a difference between those who are clean and unclean. I shall purge the one and strengthen the other. And, as I do this, do not be angry, for I am commanded to do so. Amen."

Just so, I think. *We have been lax too long, tolerating the unbelievers in our midst. It is past time to root them out.*

C H A P T E R

Reverend Samuel Parris

November 18, 1691
Salem Village Parsonage

"Shall ye light a small fire in the front room?" my wife asks, fretting about the hospitality we're scheduled to provide Deacon Putnam and others on this day. "It's quite cold."

I struggle to conceal my grimace. "Last month, the rates committee voted not to pay me this year nor to collect the firewood which is owed to us. Consequently, we eat porridge and have only the kitchen fire to warm us," I remind her. "They can keep their coats on, as we do."

"Perhaps they do not realize—"

I raise my hand to stop Elizabeth's protests. "Ye have a forgiving nature, Mistress Parris. I informed them we had hardly any wood to burn. Deacons Ingersoll and Putnam met with them and said the same, but the members refused to consider any requests unless I and the church sent them a written notice. They deflect. They protest. But they do not fulfill the terms of our agreement. I share Jehovah's scripture with them every day, yet their actions disrespect both Jehovah and myself." I shake my head in sorrow. "I fear the day Jehovah unleashes his wrath upon them."

111

Elizabeth pulls her shawl more closely around her shoulders. Her lips clench in a thin line. "Ye must exhort them more forcefully. *Make* them understand the harm they commit."

I hear a soft knocking at the kitchen entry.

"Good day." Deacon Tom Putnam stands just inside the room. "We are here, if it is convenient for ye to meet with us."

I close my prayer book. "Yes, Deacon Putnam. We are well met."

I escort Deacon Putnam into the front parlor, glancing pointedly at the empty hearth in the front room.

"Gentlemen," I say, shaking hands with Deacon Putnam, Thomas Wilkins, and Nathaniel Putnam in sequence. "Please be seated."

A gust of wind blows up and rattles the windowpanes.

I rub my hands together.

"There's a definite chill in the air today. Rest assured, I did not call this meeting without a reason, especially since I cannot offer ye the warmth of a fire on such a crisp day." I pause and glance again at the empty hearth. "I appreciate yer commitment to our church, especially since attendance at several church meetings has been poor. In fact, only three members were present at the last meeting."

Tom Putnam rubs the back of his neck, something I have noticed he often does when he's uncomfortable with a topic under discussion. The others sit with blank expressions.

"As I recall," Tom says, "it was a bitterly cold day with substantial snow. It's difficult for those living outside the central village to travel under such conditions. I daresay that could explain why attendance was down."

My temper rises, but I wrestle it into submission.

"At that time, I told those present I had barely enough wood to last until the next day. Ye can see by the stone-cold hearth before ye what action they took. Which is to say—none. My family suffers from yer neglect," I tell them, and the room goes silent.

"What would ye have us do, Reverend Parris?" Tom finally asks. "We are not authorized to collect the rates from the village."

"I propose that the three of ye petition the county court and complain about the committee's neglect of its commitments. Not only do they dishonor their contract with me, but they fail to maintain the meetinghouse. The windows are broken and covered with boards; the building is dark as well as cold. The parsonage lands are also neglected with fences in need of repair."

"Aye," Tom says. "And what remedy do we request?"

"We *request*," I say with some emphasis, "that the court order the rates committee to explain why the contract lapsed last July without any effort to compensate their ordained minister. We have a commitment between us stronger than a paper agreement, and now they must be held accountable. And ye men, representing the church, must make this appeal."

Thomas Putnam, the Younger

November 22, 1691, Sabbath
Salem Village Meetinghouse

My daughter Ann sits with one-year-old Timothy in her arms, the pair of them beside my wife in the third row of pews. Young Thomas keeps an eye on Elizabeth while my wife sits with six-year-old Ebenezer and his younger sister Deliverance, keeping them quiet and amused. At the moment, Deliverance has a tear falling from her eye. *I wonder what that's about.*

While Reverend Parris interprets the day's lesson on Psalm 110, my mind wanders. I feel an unusual sense of gratitude for my station in life. I achieved the rank of lieutenant in the militia and still have some standing in the village. My half-brother, Joseph—more viper than true brother—lives in town with his wife, seldom venturing to the village. Still, no matter where he lives, I'll never forgive him for stealing my inheritance.

"The Lord said unto my Lord, sit thou at my right hand until I make thine enemies thy footstool." Reverend Parris sets aside his Bible and looks at the congregation. I can't help but flinch at the reverend's expression of barely concealed anger. It's wrong for a reverend to allow his emotions to run away with him. "The first verse of this psalm is a consolation for the faithful," he says, "those who follow Jehovah's will. The question is, what does this mean for us here in Salem Village?"

People fidget from the cold as Reverend Parris continues his exhortation about God's comfort for the faithful and revenge for those who are Christ's enemies.

I grit my teeth to prevent them from chattering. I turn over the hourglass.

"Concerning the intercession of Christ, many things will fall under our consideration, but because of the coldness and shortness of the day, I shall leave them to another season."

Reverend Parris raises his arms for the blessing. When he reaches the last "amen," people stand, stamp their feet, and make their way out of the cold meeting house to Ingersoll's Ordinary and a place near the roaring fire in the great room.

Betty Parris

Late December 1691
Salem Village Parsonage Kitchen

"*Please*, Tituba! Show us who we will marry! I want someone who has lots of firewood," Abigail pleads.

Tituba shakes her head. "Nuh, ma'am. Massa don' like Tituba do such things. Tol' me an' John it be devil worship."

Devil worship?

I pull Abigail's sleeve.

"We can play cat's cradle instead," I whisper.

"No, why should we? Yer parents aren't here. And Tituba won't say anything, will ye?"

"Ah'll git ye string," Tituba says.

"No." Abigail stamps her foot. "I want to know who I'll marry. Tell me what to do, or I'll tell Aunt Parris ye told our fortunes."

"Don't! She'll get in trouble," I murmur.

"I'll show her trouble if she doesn't show me who we'll marry. I want someone rich. Well, Tituba, will ye show us?"

Tituba pulls a tankard out of the cupboard. She fills it with water and places it on the table in front of Abigail near the last coals in the fire.

"Don' wanna change yer mind?"

"No. Show me now."

Tituba hands Abigail an egg and a shallow bowl. "Crack de egg, take out de yolk, an' pour da rest in da water," she instructs, and Abigail taps the egg three times before drawing the shell apart.

I watch, my heart thumping against my chest.

Abigail tosses the two halves of the egg's contents back and forth until the yolk remains in one of the shell halves and the white fills the bowl.

"'Tip it in da water," Tituba says.

Abigail pours the bowl's contents into the tankard, where it swirls to form ghostly patterns that eventually form into an oblong shape.

"What's that?" I ask Abigail.

"I don't know," she says, but it seems clear Tituba does. The woman clutches her chest and turns away, praying to angels for mercy.

Abigail, her eyes like saucers, reaches for my hand. "Do ye see it?"

I shake my head. After a moment, I see a white shape that looks like a coffin I saw once when our family visited the house where someone died. I gasp, unable to get my breath. "It's like . . . it's like where a dead person's body goes. 'Member?"

"Aye," Abigail exclaims. "It's a coffin! Ye're right. I'll marry death, and the devil's going to kill us both."

I start screaming uncontrollably. So does Abigail.

Tituba grabs the tankard and throws the contents outside. "Ain' no debbil. S'nuthin!" she says, as if she weren't only moments ago praying in fear. "Stop wailin'. Yer folks be home soon. Don' let 'em see ye like dis."

I run out of the kitchen and into our bedroom upstairs, screaming so loudly I feel sick. Abigail runs at my heels. I kneel by my bed, clasping my hands in prayer.

"I'm sorry!" I wail to Jehovah. "I didn't mean it!"

Nothing happens.

"Jehovah will punish us," I whisper to Abigail.

"Not if we say we're sorry. Say it again!"

"I already said I was sorry."

"Do it *again*, for both of us."

"Mighty Jehovah," I whisper. "We sinned, and we repent. Please forgive us. Amen." I start crying again.

"Ye can't tell anyone what we did," Abigail says. "Swear ye won't."

"I do."

"Good, because if ye do, I'll pinch ye until ye're black and blue."

"I won't tell anyone. I promise."

Elizabeth Parris

January 1692
Salem Village Parsonage Kitchen

My niece, Abigail, shrieks and writhes on the floor while clutching her head. I rush to calm her and hold the girl tightly, but she continues to moan.

"What's happening to ye, Abigail? How have ye hurt yerself?" I ask her, frightened.

"Someone hits me! I can't bear it!"

"Abigail, no one is here."

"There's someone. Betty, ye tell her."

"Tell me what?" I ask my daughter, but Betty, eyes wide, just shakes her head.

"I don't know," she whispers. "I'm sorry."

"For what?"

"I don't know!" Betty shrieks and begins running around the kitchen table.

"I can't bear the pain," Abigail moans.

In the corner, Tituba watches the uproar while shaking her head vehemently. I hold Abigail's arms against her body and pick up the now rigid girl. Betty crawls under the table and begins chanting gibberish while I hold Abigail in my lap and begin rocking her.

"Betty," I say, "come out from under the table."

But Betty curls into a ball instead.

Reverend Parris enters the kitchen, bundled in his coat and scarf. "What is all this noise, Mistress Parris? I can hear it in my study, and I must tell ye it is most upsetting."

"It is more upsetting to be *here*," I say, more forcefully than I should. "The girls are beside themselves! Abigail insists someone is hitting her. Betty won't come out from under the table. Tituba is hiding in the corner. Something is very wrong."

Reverend Parris leans over to see Betty under the table. He extends his hand. "Betty, I insist that ye come out this instant! Yer behavior is an offense against yer parents and against Jehovah. I've explained what Jehovah does to bad children. Now take my hand and come out of there."

Betty scoots out from the opposite side of the table, only to resume her earlier behavior of shrieking while running around the room. Reverend Parris grabs his daughter by the arm, halting her at once, and yet the girl continues to struggle. Even he is mystified. This isn't the behavior of an ill-tempered child. It's something else, I'm sure of it.

"Look at her face, Reverend Parris!" I say, still rocking Abigail. "Her eyes are open but have no focus. Could she be . . ." *Possessed by an evil spirit?*

I don't need to say the rest. Reverend Parris knows what I'm getting at. His face hardens at the mere suggestion. "Decidedly not! She is willful and disobedient. I'm taking her to her bed. Follow me with Abigail."

I hold on to Abigail and stand. Betty wails all the way up the stairs. Reverend Parris places her in her bed and swaddles her in blankets. Betty begins whimpering.

"There, now." I reach around my husband to stroke Betty's head. "Ye are safe here under Jehovah's protection. Close yer eyes."

I gently close Betty's eyelids, the way one might a corpse's, and turn to place Abigail in her own bed. The girl's limbs become less rigid, but she's still not herself. Her eyes are locked open in absolute terror.

"Look, husband," I whisper, desperate for him to see what I'm seeing. "Abigail has the same glaze over her eyes as Betty! What can we do for them?"

"We shall pray and seek what remedy we may find. Speak to no one about their condition. We don't want unfounded rumors to spread." Reverend Parris wraps blankets securely around Abigail and reaches for my hand. "Come, we shall pray for Jehovah to take this disease from us."

Sarah Good

February 1692
Road to Salem Village

The wealthy keep their fancy houses near the village center. The Putnams. The Walcotts. All of them with snug houses and plenty to eat. I despise them, each and every one. They offer charity but turn me away. They don't care if my children starve.

"Mam?"

I cringe, clutch my infant more closely, and look down at Dorothy rubbing her hand across her belly. What will it be this time? She's hungry or tired or cold. Always something.

"What do ye want, Dorothy?"

"Mam, I'm hungry."

"We took eggs from a chicken this mornin'. 'Ow can ye be hungry?"

"Because . . ." Tears well up in her eyes.

I squat down so I can look into Dorothy's dirty face. I spit on my sleeve and begin rubbing mud off my daughter's face. *Why is she always such a mess?* "I don't know why ye always look like ye live in dirt." I blot off what I can. "That's better. I kin see yer bonny face again."

"Mam . . ."

I hold up my hand. "Dinna start, poppet. We'll go to these houses and beg for food. Jehovah said it's good to help the poor, and we be poor an' all."

I adjust little Mercy's sling and hold out my hand to Dorothy.

"We'll begin at the preacher's house."

I pat down my clothes and adjust my hat before I approach the kitchen door at the back of the parsonage. My husband can't provide for us. If it wasn't for the children, I think I might lay by the side of the road and die. I squeeze Dorothy's shoulder and gather my courage.

Reverend Samuel Parris

February 1692
Salem Village Parsonage Kitchen

From my seat near the kitchen fire, I continue documenting Betty and Abigail's strange behavior in my journal. It's important to record everything happening, so I can determine if an evil spirit does indeed threaten my household. Lucifer is very bold to attack Jehovah through his servant.

My two servants—Tituba and her husband, Indian John—are also acting strangely.

My niece and older daughter see things I, my wife, and my older son do not. Betty and Abigail are not responding to prayers, admonitions, discipline, or any other means of control.

Outside, the wind whips around, spewing snow everywhere. Inside, the house remains stone cold. For a moment, the wind drops, and I hear a faint rapping at the door. Tituba starts to answer, but I hold up my hand.

"I'll go."

I crack the kitchen door open. "Yes?"

There is a woman outside. She is slovenly and emaciated. No doubt one of the creatures without a fixed abode. She holds an infant strapped to her chest by her shawl. Next to her is a small girl without an outer coat. The wind blows the girl's light hair across her face.

Why doesn't she have a hat?

The woman curtsies and keeps her eyes on the ground.

"Forgive me, Master," she says in a gravelly voice. "Expected yer girl ta open da door."

I give the woman a cold stare. She'll have no welcome here. "What brings ye to my door?"

"Hunger, Yer Worship. Ain't got nuthin' ta eat. Grant us a favor," the woman whines.

I search my heart and find it bare. I have no patience with vagrants and beggars. Yet, I look at the girl standing beside her mother. The child is innocent—and clearly starving, freezing, and quite unlikely to survive the winter without help.

"Does she have a name?" I ask.

"Dorothy, Master. I've no clothing for her, an' it be cold." The woman pulls her threadbare coat closer to her body.

I turn away from the door. "Betty," I call, "bring me yer coat."

"What are ye doing, husband?" Elizabeth asks.

"Practicing Christian charity. It is not the child's fault her mother is a slattern."

Betty hands me her coat. I shake it out and turn back to the doorway.

"Ye there, girl . . . Dorothy. Put this on."

The child wraps the coat around her. The woman watches and holds her fingers to her lips. Elizabeth comes up behind me with a small loaf of bread. I give it to the woman.

"Shelter elsewhere," I order, "and earn yer way properly."

"Properly. Aye. Thankee fer yer kindness, Master." The woman curtsies. "Come, Dorothy."

The woman mutters as she walks away, but whether she voices a blessing or a curse, I cannot tell.

Reverend Samuel Parris

February 1692
Salem Village Parsonage

My study is a gloomy space on a cold winter's day. The small diamond-paned window rattles when the wind strikes it. I could close the curtain and block the draft, but I decide to suffer the cold and leave it open against the darkness that surrounds me.

I clasp my hands and take a deep breath, opening a dialogue with the master of my life.

"Mighty and everlasting Jehovah . . ."

I don't want to confess my shortcomings—the disarray of my household and my inability to bring my stiff-necked congregation into a right relationship with Jehovah—and yet confession is exactly what I must do.

"I am weak," I admit. "I fall short. I pray for my insensible daughter, but ye send her no relief. I beg ye not to punish her for my shortcomings."

My thoughts drift. I remember the way Jesus healed the daughter of Jairus. Jesus told the grieving father to *believe*, and his daughter would be made whole. And so she was.

I clench my jaw.

"Forgive my lack of faith," I plead. "The fault is not Betty's but mine. Take these invisible tortures from her. I beg ye."

I stand in stillness, hoping to feel Jehovah's compassion, but the room remains dark and silent.

"Amen," I breathe.

My heartfelt prayer brings no sense of comfort, only a severe sense of shame for my shortcomings that is quickly followed by righteous anger.

It is time to separate the sheep from the goats.

Thomas Putnam, the Younger

February 14, 1692
Salem Village Meetinghouse

Outside the meetinghouse door, I stamp my boots to knock the snow and slush off their soles. My older daughter and son do the same. The rest of my family remain snug at home, gathered around the hearth as they nurse sniffles and coughs. I once thought the scorching fires of hell were the worst possible challenge to the human spirit—now, I wonder if perhaps bone-chilling cold is even more formidable.

Escorting my family to their seats, I note more than a few people absent. Usually, the meetinghouse is full on Sundays when the Lord's Supper is served. I watch my daughter take her seat, then take my son to the men's side of the room.

Reverend Parris enters the meetinghouse from the side door. He wears a thick cassock and gloves. His wife, similarly bundled against the cold, sits in the first row with her infant Susannah, who is wrapped in a shawl and clasped against her chest. I take my place in front. After the opening prayers and psalms, I pick up the hourglass and prepare to turn it when Reverend Parris begins speaking.

Reverend Parris stands for several minutes, as if gathering his thoughts.

"This is," he begins, "the last of three Sabbath Day sermons on Psalm 110, verse 1. 'The Lord said unto my Lord, sit thou at my right hand, until I make thine enemies thy footstool.' We have spoken of the exaltation of our wounded and bruised Mediator, and of his ascension into heaven, where he sits at the right hand of God.

"Now it is time to speak of the fruits of his ascension, which are Christ's intercession for believers, and the way he governs and defends his church by subduing people's lusts and defending their grace. The devil may try to pluck them away, but he shall not succeed."

I turn the hourglass and settle further into my seat. I assume full church membership makes me a member of the Elect, destined for heaven and safe from the devil's lure. But am I? And if being a member of the church doesn't save me, what will?

"Ministers are called to separate the precious and the vile to gather a pure church for Christ," Reverend Parris exhorts from the pulpit. "Those who subject themselves to Christ's laws, we accept, and to them we offer comfort, but we reject those who do not. If we would reign with Christ, we must subdue our spiritual enemies. And so we are not offended at the present low condition of the church, which is surrounded by enemies. Soon, it shall be otherwise."

Ah, I think, *clearly Reverend Parris still smarts from the dissenters among us.*

"Christ governs his church by his word and spirit, and also by his rod and afflictions. So we must not faint when we are chastised. It is done for our profit." Reverend Parris pauses and drops his voice. "The church may meet with storms, but it shall never sink, because Christ takes care of his little ship bound for the port of heaven, laden with the treasure purchased by his blood. Thus ye have no cause to fear."

As the last grain of sand falls through the hourglass, I stretch in my seat and stand for the blessing. Reverend Parris raises his hands before the congregation of shivering listeners.

"The Lord, bless thee and keep thee. The Lord maketh his face to shine upon thee and be gracious unto thee. The Lord lift up his countenance upon thee and give thee peace."

Mumbled "amens" sound as people turn to leave the meetinghouse. I collect my children and head for Ingersoll's Ordinary. They need to warm up by the great fire before the walk home.

Abigail Williams

February 25, 1692
Salem Village Parsonage

"Are ye sure ye don't mind yer uncle and I attending Thursday Lecture?" my aunt asks me as she kneels beside my chair. I haven't felt well since that January night when Tituba tried to foresee my future, but I'm not about to tell Aunt Parris that. "If ye're unwell, I can stay here with ye while yer uncle attends."

My head aches all the time now—more so when my aunt constantly watches me. "I'll be as well as ever. There's nothing ye can do. Ye should go. Uncle Parris will be displeased if ye stay behind."

My aunt looks undecided.

Reverend Parris holds out his wife's thick coat. "Come. The children are fine."

"Yes, very well."

My aunt kisses her daughter before taking her husband's arm and departing for the next town.

I wait until I hear the door close—the sound of footsteps fading as my aunt and uncle walk out of earshot—and even a few more minutes, to be safe. When I'm sure they're gone, I say, "Hurry, Tituba! We want to make the cake before they return." I leap up to my feet. "Betty, come stand by me so we can watch what Tituba does."

I walk toward the kitchen table and put my arm around Betty's shoulders.

Tituba shakes her head. "Ah dunno. Massa don' like magic."

"But it's the only way we can stop our misery!" I insist, near tears. "And Mistress Sibley gave ye the recipe. I have our urine."

Tituba's eyes widen.

I pass her a glass vial. "Do it," I order. "Ye got us into this, Tituba. Now ye've got to get us out of it."

With a sigh, Tituba puts rye meal into a bowl and adds the urine I collected from the chamber pot Betty and I share. She mixes the ingredients together and shapes a small loaf that resembles unbaked bread.

"Dat look right ta ye, John?" Tituba asks her husband, who nods.

"Put 'em in da ashes to bake," he says.

An hour later, Tituba lifts the loaf out of the fire. After it cools, I open the kitchen door.

"Rosco," I call. The dog comes to me, wagging his tail. "Come inside. I have something for ye."

"Dog's gonna make a mess," John says.

"I'm not standing in the wind to feed the dog." I put the cake on the floor, pleased when Rosco immediately consumes it. I motion for Betty to sit on the floor with me. "We'll have to watch Rosco closely to see what happens."

"Look!" Betty points only a second later. "I see someone near the hearth!"

"Who?"

"She's the one who pinches me!"

"Let me look."

Tituba and John sit in a dark corner of the kitchen. I look around the kitchen again, straining my eyes to see what Betty saw.

"Is it like a person, but in haze?"

Betty nods her head.

I think I must be dreaming. My head hurts and someone pinches me

Tituba touches my shoulder. "Got ta put da dog out now. An' git offen da floor. Rev'rend be back soon."

Reluctantly, Rosco goes back outside.

Betty and I take seats near the kitchen fire and stare into the coals, our minds distracted by all the possibilities of what we've done today. Mistress Sibley was sure this witch cake would protect us from evil spirits, but I'm not so sure. I don't feel any differently. My head still hurts with a sharp pain.

The kitchen door opens, letting in a strong draft.

"We're home, darlings!" my aunt says.

"We saw them," Betty replies.

"Saw who?"

"The people who hurt us."

"In a dream?" my aunt asks.

My uncle places his hat near the door as he enters. "How now? What has upset ye, Mistress Parris?"

"The girls," she says. "They say they saw the spirits who hurt them."

My uncle's face blanches. "How is that possible? Who is it?"

I shake my head in fear. "We only saw shapes. We don't know who it is."

"And how did ye come to see these shapes?"

I look at Tituba's panicked face and scream.

"I don't know!" I point at an empty space. "But it was there! I saw it!"

Thomas Putnam, the Younger

February 27, 1692
Tom Putnam's House

My sense of panic recedes as I watch Ann nurse our youngest son. She sits by the fire, her face momentarily relaxed from the day's cares. But I can't let my guard down. Rumors of recent events at the parsonage are chilling. If Reverend Parris's family can be caught up in such inexplicable events, what hope does the village have to survive? I want to ask my wife what she thinks of it all, but I can't bear to disrupt her peace.

My oldest daughter rushes into the room, her eyes madly searching for something.

"Stop it! Stop pinching me! I won't sign yer book!" she shrieks.

"Ann—*Ann!*" my wife cries while detaching Timothy from her breast in such haste I fear she'll harm herself. "Take him," she says, passing the wailing infant to me in order to see to our thirteen-year-old daughter. The girl goes rigid, eyes wide with fear, and seems to stare at something just over our shoulder—something we decidedly cannot see.

"There's no one here, child. Ye are safe," I tell Ann. My wife looks to me, bewildered and afraid, and I find I struggle to shake off my own fears. I know better, and yet I keep looking over my shoulder, following Ann's line of vision.

To nothing. Nothing is there.

My daughter jumps to her feet, waving her arms. "Can't ye see her? Ye must see her! She's just there!" This time, she points to the fire.

"No one is here, Ann!" I snap. "Ye must stop this nonsense."

Ann's arm twists up her back and she moans, as though being tortured.

How can I save my beautiful, sweet daughter?

"Who is it that torments ye? Tell me!" I demand to know.

"She named herself *Goody Good*." Ann gasps. "Owwww! Make her stop, Papa! Please make her stop!"

"Where is she now? Is she still here?"

Ann shakes her head. "She's gone now."

I rack my brain for the cause of Ann's suffering. Reverend Parris spoke of enemies surrounding our church, and I realize these events can only be the devil's work.

"I'm going to the court," I announce. "I'm filing warrants against members of what I'm sure is an entire nest of witches. We will put them on trial and execute them for their crimes. Ye will be safe again, Ann. I swear it."

Elizabeth Hubbard

February 27, 1692
Salem Village

A biting wind rushes across the Common, lashing my face with raindrops. I pull down my hat to protect my face. My aunt won't send her daughter out in this weather, but she doesn't hesitate to send me.

I'm her kin, and she treats me like a servant. Says I'm lucky to have a home.

I keep my grievances close to my chest. I can't afford to be thrown out of the house, because I have what she calls a *willful disposition.*

The wind curls around me like a living thing. A wailing sound fills the air.

Can it be a wolf? I banish the silly thought. Hunters drove the wolves out of the village years ago. But what if Goody Good sent a wolf to harass me or became one herself so she can force me to sign her book? Abigail told me all about Sarah Good. My heart thuds, and I pick up my pace. Perhaps the wolf just wants to scare me and won't actually attack.

Without warning, I feel something strike my shoulder. *It's Sarah Good! I know it is!*

I scramble across the uneven ground to reach the Griggs's house as quickly as possible.

The house comes into my view, and suddenly the wind shifts direction.

I pull open the kitchen door, slamming it behind me. My chest is heaving, and my shoulder throbs so much I lean against the door for support.

"What's happened to ye?" Rachel Griggs asks.

"The witch!" I gasp. "She tried to make me sign her book, but I ran away!"

Magistrate John Hathorne

February 29, 1692
Salem Town Courthouse

The headache presses against the back of my forehead, an invader that destroys my peace. I press my fingers onto my temple, willing the pain to recede. All day, the wind has howled, whistled, and blown things about without respite while petitioners plead their cases and complaints. I long to adjourn the court and return home to eat a meal with my family.

"What do ye think, Master Corwin?" I ask while the clerk draws up a document. "Is it time to close court for the day?"

My brother-in-law nods. "We've spent enough time on the town's business and not enough on our own."

We put aside our pens.

"A moment, Yer Worships," the court clerk says. "Four men just arrived from the village. They request a warrant against several women they think are witches."

"Witches?" I say with a quiet scoff. "The village must be in greater confusion than usual."

"There must be something to it if they walked all the way here in this weather. We'd better hear their complaint," Corwin replies. "Constables, do ye know anything about this?"

Constables Locker and Herrick shake their heads.

"The village has been pretty quiet," Locker says, "though there is a rumor of witch possession at Reverend Parris's house."

"Really?" The thought of witches causing havoc so close to town is worrisome, especially in the reverend's home. "Show them in."

Constable Locker leaves the room, returning with four village men a few minutes later. Corwin looks at them with distaste as they track mud into the room, their faces red from the wind and lips chapped by the chill.

"Weather is still blowing up, I see," Corwin says.

"Aye, that it is," Tom Putnam responds. "I'm here with my brother, Edward Putnam, Thomas Preston, and Joseph Hutchinson to request a warrant for the arrest of the vagrant Sarah Good, the invalid recluse Sarah Osborne, and Reverend Parris's slave, Tituba."

I lean forward over the table, taken aback. "Explain yer complaint."

"I can scarcely believe what I'm about to tell ye, but 'tis true. Witches are practicing their evil ways in the village, and we need to arrest them before the contagion spreads further. Events began at Reverend Parris's house when his daughter and niece began behaving strangely. The disorder reached a point so severe, he called in neighboring clergy to pray with them."

"I remember Reverend Noyes saying something about that," Corwin says, turning to address me in a low voice. "He said the girls' contortions and babbling struck fear into his soul. He did not say it was witchcraft, however."

"Nay," Putnam responds before continuing his tale. "The clergy had no idea what the trouble was and advised fasting and prayer until Jehovah responded. We held fast days and group prayer, but the girls continued to suffer. Reverend Parris called in Dr. Griggs. He suggested the girls were under an evil hand. But we had no idea how that occurred until finally the girls began naming their tormentors."

I look up from the notes I'm taking. "And who are they?"

"Reverend Parris's daughter and niece named Sarah Good and Tituba as the ones who appeared to them and pinched them."

"Who is this Sarah Good?" Corwin asks, brows furrowed.

"A vagrant and beggar of no account," Tom Putnam says. "Her husband William is a common laborer. Stories have circulated about Goody Good before, but nothing so dire. The worst events happened on Saturday when my daughter and Dr. Griggs's niece, Elizabeth Hubbard, were both afflicted by Sarah Good, and Elizabeth said Goody Osborne also afflicted her. This contagion is spreading into the village. It must be stopped before we're all swept up in a maelstrom of witchery. These three are clearly the vanguard of the devil's legion."

"I agree," I say. "We must stop the contagion immediately. Do ye not agree, Master Corwin?"

"I agree."

"Clerk, prepare two warrants. The first warrant is for the arrest of Sarah Good, the wife of William Good, to be administered by Constable Locker. The second, against the invalid Sarah Osborne, wife of Alexander Osborne, and Tituba, an Indian woman and servant of Reverend Samuel Parris, to be administered by Constable Herrick," I say, completing my notes. "They are to be apprehended and brought before us tomorrow at ten o' clock in the morning at the house of Lieutenant Nathaniel Ingersoll in Salem Village to be examined on suspicion of witchcraft against Elizabeth Parris, Abigail Williams, Ann Putnam, and Elizabeth Hubbard at sundry times during the past two months.

"Constable Locker, ye will locate and arrest Sarah Good. Constable Herrick, ye will arrest Sarah Osborne and Tituba. Constable Herrick, ye are also to bring Elizabeth Parris, Abigail Williams, Ann Putnam, and Elizabeth Hubbard to court, and any other person that can give evidence. Gentlemen, ye are not to fail in these endeavors. Wait until the clerk has finished the warrants and be about yer business. We shall see ye with yer prisoners tomorrow at ten o'clock."

I return my attention to the four men standing before me.

"I trust our actions satisfy yer complaint."

"Aye, Master Hathorne," Tom Putnam says. "We are grateful for yer efforts."

I nod my dismissal. "Go back to yer homes and leave the court's business to us."

The clerk finishes writing the warrants and passes them to us for our signatures. I sign with a flourish, Corwin with slightly less flamboyance.

"Do we have to hold the examinations in the village tomorrow morning—in this weather? The journey will be taxing," Corwin complains.

"But well worth the trouble. We cannot allow a witch even one extra day to wield the devil's magic. Prepare to stay the week." I get to my feet. "And now, I'm off home for my dinner."

"Meet me at my house at seven o' clock, and we'll travel down together," Corwin grumbles.

"Until tomorrow." I put on my coat and hat before opening the door to a chill gust of wind. I hope my discomfort isn't an omen of coming events.

Constable George Locker

March 1, 1692
Countryside Near Salem Village

I wrap the court's warrant in oilskin and place it in my coat pocket. I need to bring the woman to Ingersoll's before ten o'clock, but despite knowing Goody Good wanders in and out of the village on a frequent basis, I don't know exactly where to look for her in order to issue the arrest warrant. The arrest itself is unsettling. I never took her for a witch, just a beggar woman half out of her mind from hunger and grief and rough living.

I walk about half a mile before I spy a bit of movement in the meadow next to the road. That could be her in the distance. I leave the road and lengthen my stride.

"Ye! Ye there! Stop!" I shout.

The figure pauses and holds a hand over her eyes, shading them from the bright overcast sky to look in my direction. I lengthen my stride until I'm only a few feet away.

The figure wasn't that of a woman but a girl. I ask her, "Do ye know Goody Good?"

"Dat's me mam," the child answers. *What luck.* "She's over there by the tree."

I look to the tree. Lo and behold, Goody Good is there.

"Stay where ye are!" I say, though she in such a terrible state, I don't think she could run away if she tried. Ragged clothing hangs off her emaciated body. Her cheeks are sunken, and her skin is raw from the wind. The child walks up to us. She is carrying an infant small enough to be a doll. I feel a pang of pity and harden my heart.

"Wot ye want wid me?" the woman asks in a rough, apathetic voice.

"Are ye Sarah Good?"

"Dat's me name. Wot's it to ye?"

"Do ye know who I am?"

The woman shakes her head. "Nay."

"I'm Constable Locker. I have a warrant for yer arrest."

"Fer wot?"

"Ye are charged with witchcraft."

The woman drops her mouth open in surprise. "Wot? Why? Ahm no witch!"

"The warrant says ye practiced witchcraft to injure Betty Parris, Abigail Williams, Ann Putnam, and Elizabeth Hubbard."

Sarah snorts and pulls out her pipe. "I never did. Got tabak fer ma pipe?"

I shake my head in refusal.

She shrugs and puts the empty pipe in her mouth.

"The magistrates will examine ye to decide if ye are a witch or not. Ye need to come with me."

"Can't leave da babe," she says simply.

"I'll bring yer children along and send for yer husband to take them."

Sarah laughs. "Mercy stays wid me," she says, nodding to the infant. "Got ta feed 'er."

I reach for Sarah's arm. "If ye don't come willingly, I'll drag ye."

"Leave off," she snaps, pulling away. "We'll come."

Sarah Good

March 1, 1692
Walking to Ingersoll's Ordinary

Constable Locker wraps his fist around my arm. Must think I'll run away, but I canna escape. I wince against his tight grip.

"Dinna need ta hold me! Said we go wid ye!" I twist to break his grip. No luck.

"The warrant says ye appeared to folk. Ye won't get away from me."

I shake my head in annoyance, watching Dorothy stumble on the path back to the road.

"Lemme hold me babe!" I say. "Girl'll drop 'er."

"Very well." Locker stops.

I secure my shawl and hold out my arms. "Giv 'er here, Dorothy, an' keep up or ye'll be lost."

I take my time securing Mercy, tightening the shawl to hold her head steady. Locker grabs my upper arm again and half drags me to the road. The footing is easier on the smoother surface.

"Where we goin'?" I ask.

"The ordinary. The magistrates will ask ye questions. I advise ye to be truthful."

My mind buzzes. Magistrates dinna rule in my favor. They gave my father's inheritance to my mother, and then took what little remained from what I finally got. Now I only have hungry mouths to feed.

"I dinna have anythin' left fer dem to take. What dey want wid me?"

"They want the *truth*. They want to know if ye tormented children."

"Never did nuthin' ta children."

Locker doesn't answer.

After an hour of steady walking, we arrive at the village. Immense crowds watch us walk into Ingersoll's Ordinary. People always stare at me before looking away, usually with disgust. But now everyone in the crowd watches me with peculiar fascination. I growl at them, enjoying this small shift in power. I find it is nicer to be feared by them than feel like dirt under their boots.

Inside the ordinary, I smell the mouthwatering scent of the kitchen. Roasting meat. Onions. Something savory. I salivate. *Mayhap dey'll feed us.*

"Goodwife Ingersoll, where shall I leave the prisoner?"

"Leave the children with the barmaid and put the witch in the back room. The other two are there already. My daughter and I will be in shortly," she says.

"Dorothy," Locker says. "Take yer sister and wait out here."

"What about Mam?"

"She goes in the back room with the others."

I shake my head and clutch Mercy closer. "Nay, ye canna take ma girls."

Locker unties my shawl, wraps it around the baby, and gives the bundle to Dorothy. I watch as my eldest daughter sits down on a bench and jiggles her knee so Mercy doesn't cry. I feel hot tears fill my eyes. They can't seriously think I'm a *witch*!

I try to twist my way out of Locker's grip, but he only holds me tighter.

"Ye've no right!" I shout and begin to wail.

"I'm the constable. I have *all* the rights. And ye are going in here," Locker says, shoving me into a dark storeroom.

I land on all fours and look around. Boxes and barrels are stacked against the walls of the cramped room. It's freezing. The door is closed in my face and locked for good measure, and I hear the voices outside fade.

"Dorothy!" I scream, pounding my fists on the door. "Mercy!"

"Try not to worry, my dear," I hear a voice say from behind me. My heart pounds, and I clutch the pipe in my pocket for comfort. "Over here. Look on yer left, in front of the barrels."

An old woman sits on a stool and leans her back against the wall.

"Who are ye?" I ask softly.

"Sarah Osborne. And I know ye're Sarah Good. Come closer. It's hard for me to speak."

I scoot across the floor. "Wot dey want wid us?"

"They think we're witches. Someone will search us for witch's marks. They won't find any."

"Then we leave?"

"Probably not. Magistrates are coming from town, and people are here to watch them."

My vision starts to narrow. I feel blood rushing to my head. They're going to pin the blame on us for something.

Goody Osborne points to a dark figure on the other side of the room. "That's Tituba over there. The girls' torments started with her."

"She a witch?"

"I don't know." The woman looks to the shadowy corner. "Tituba, are ye a witch?"

The dark-skinned woman shakes her head vigorously.

I sit next to Goody Osborne. The woman closes her eyes, exhausted.

For the first time, I'm afraid. *Terrified*, more like. I can't be a witch—not unless it's possible to be a witch *accidentally*. If I really am a witch, I don't think I'd be poor.

The door opens, letting in light and noise from the tavern great room. Hannah Ingersoll and her daughter bustle into the back room, letting the door close again. Hannah carries a lantern that casts a soft, buttery light into the cold, dim room.

"We're here to inspect ye for witch's marks. All of ye, take off yer clothing," Hannah says. "Quickly, or I'll have the constables assist ye. Sarah Good, ye have less to remove, so I'll check ye first."

"Nay, ye won't see me," I say, shrinking away.

Hannah puts her hands on her ample hips and glares at me. "If ye don't cooperate, I'll bring the constables in to rip yer clothes off. I've better things to do than examine yer body."

Slowly, I remove my outer wear and stand in my shift.

"Stand in the center of the room."

I comply and lower my eyes as one woman holds the lamp while the other draws off my shift. They inspect every inch of my body, including my secret parts.

"Well," Hannah says, at last, "if ye are a witch, the devil couldn't be bothered to mark his claim. Get dressed."

I used to think falling into vagrancy was the worst thing that ever happened to me, but it wasn't. I watch the women carefully look at every inch of each of my companions and feel an increasing sense of dread. The inspectors agree none of us have witch's marks. But somehow, I don't think their conclusion will make much difference.

Hannah Ingersoll pauses by the door.

"They'll examine ye separately," she says. "Keep a civil tongue in yer heads and answer their questions. They came all the way from town this morning, so they'll be looking fer a reason for their inconvenience."

Magistrate John Hathorne

March 1, 1692
On the Road to Salem Village

"It's a good thing ye ordered the prisoners delivered at ten o'clock," Jonathan Corwin says as we travel on horseback to the village. We're not there yet and it's well past ten, though I'm certain our trek won't be for much longer. "It would be inefficient if we had to wait for them."

I purse my lips. *Is he mocking me?*

"I ordered the prisoners to be delivered at ten; I didn't say court would *convene* by that point in time," I tell him. "The women need time to search for witch's marks."

"Ye're correct, of course." Corwin gestures to the road ahead. "Looks like we have an escort the rest of the way into the village."

I gaze at the crowd waiting near the side of the road and take a moment to study them. I'd prefer to ride into the village and get straight to business, but clearly people expect some sort of promenade. I recognize the village marshal, two local constables, and members of the militia holding flags. Also a drummer who, judging from the noise drifting across the road, is clearly practicing a sort of rolling sound.

Lieutenant Putnam catches sight of us and rides his bay gelding in our direction.

We stop to wait for him.

"Good day, sirs. I hope ye've had a peaceful journey," he says, halting his horse a few feet away from us. The beast paws at the loose dirt underfoot, blowing steam through its nostrils. "At least the weather is dry."

"Ye didn't have to inconvenience yerselves greeting us. We could have met at Ingersoll's."

"Gentlemen, we are honored to have ye in our village, despite the unfortunate circumstances. It is our duty to welcome ye properly," Putnam says. "Come, we will escort ye the rest of the way. Deacon Ingersoll hopes ye'll take refreshments before ye call the court to order."

I nod. "Have the prisoners arrived?"

"Yes. The constables brought them in earlier this morning and secured them. Hannah Ingersoll and her daughter inspected them for witch's marks. She failed to find any. But the room was dim. Come."

Putnam turns his horse around and leads us to the waiting group.

I'm relieved when the villagers take up their formation without requiring introductions. The group moves at a brisk pace, escorting us through throngs of people lining the road. This must be quite entertaining if the farmers are willing to leave their fields. The entire atmosphere feels like a festival. *Do they not understand the seriousness of this event? Their eternal souls are in danger, yet they smile and laugh in complete confidence.*

Ingersoll's Ordinary is a substantial house, but even so, it cannot accommodate the throng of hopeful witnesses. Tables are set up outside to serve the crowd, and business is brisk. *Have they all come to witness the proceedings?*

Our cavalcade stops at the tavern's front door. Everyone dismounts, tossing their horses' reins to the stable boy. I flip the lad a small copper coin to help him remember to treat our horses well.

Nathaniel Ingersoll bustles outside. "Welcome to my humble tavern, Yer Worships. We have all in readiness for ye inside."

I survey the crowd, which has fallen silent and now presses closer to us. These people expect to see the examinations, and who knows what their response will be if they are denied. I turn my attention back to the tavern keeper.

"And will ye be able to accommodate the many people who have come to see justice done?"

"My establishment is not so large as to accommodate everyone who wishes entry, but we have room for a goodly number, perhaps fifty," he reports.

I look at the crowd. "Fifty."

"Perhaps more, if they stand close together."

"Standing."

Ingersoll looks nervous. "Yes, Yer Worship. In addition to the court, fifty people should be able to stand together and hear the proceedings. They can inform the others."

"That will not do, Deacon Ingersoll. The people have a right to witness justice being served and the scourge of witchcraft banished from this land. Do ye not agree, Master Corwin?"

"The people have that right. I suggest we remove to the meetinghouse. It can be converted while we have refreshments. I think that will suit us well."

"There is yer answer, Deacon Ingersoll," I tell him. "Prepare the meetinghouse for court proceedings while we refresh ourselves."

Reverend Samuel Parris

Two o'clock in the afternoon, March 1, 1692
Salem Village Meetinghouse

Tom Putnam forcefully opens the creaking meetinghouse door. Behind him, several men carry a long table from the ordinary on their shoulders.

"What is all this?" I demand.

"Put the table down," Tom orders. His men do as ordered, and while they position the table at the front of the room, he turns to me. "The magistrates want the examinations to be public, and the ordinary is too small for the crowd. So court will be held here."

"Here!?" My mouth drops open in shock. "But this is Jehovah's house, not a place for sundry business."

"Magistrate Hathorne is of a mind that rooting out witchcraft is part of Jehovah's business, so he'll take care of matters here. Help me move back the pulpit so we can put the table there instead. We'll put the seats for the magistrates and their secretary behind the table, facing the assembly. Put the table there, lads."

Tom gestures to the space in front of the pulpit. I watch in horror as Putnam's men transform my meetinghouse into a court of law. The pulpit is rearranged, and the table is placed there.

When the two magistrates stroll in, I rush to greet them. "Allow me to introduce myself. I am Reverend Parris," I say, bowing my head respectfully. "This is my meetinghouse."

"Good day to ye. I am your magistrate John Hathorne, and this is my colleague, Jonathan Corwin." Hathorne gestures to the man next to him. "We'll just find our seats behind the bar."

I can't decide if the man is dismissing me or just too busy to respect my position.

"Ye'll be doing the opening prayer, I presume?" Hathorne asks as he passes me by.

"Yes, Yer Worship," I say.

"Excellent. We'll proceed when everyone is seated. Please ask the constables to escort the witnesses to the first bench so they may face us. And then allow people to take their seats." He gives me a pointed look. "Don't deny *anyone* entry."

"I'll bring the witnesses," I say. "They are at my house."

"Ah, just so," Hathorne responds. He turns away, then, to introduce himself to the secretary for the proceedings.

I watch for a moment and then walk swiftly through the cold weather to my house. I find the four girls sitting in my kitchen, near the fire. One moment, they seem peaceful, and the next, they begin mumbling and contorting their bodies in all sorts of inhuman angles. My daughter cants her head like a bird, eyes rolling back in her skull, while my niece froths at her mouth, lips glossed in a thick lacquer of spit. It is an unsavory, disturbing sight, and I pray Jehovah works through these magistrates today to enact justice.

The other two girls are no better, and their families equally disturbed.

"Is it time for us to leave?" Mistress Parris asks.

I look at my wife's pale face and the dark circles under her eyes. Elizabeth isn't afflicted, as such, but she suffers as much as anyone in this crisis. To think that the instigator lived under my roof for so many years! How did she become the devil's minion?

"The examinations will be in the meetinghouse," I inform her, and she raises her brows. Before she can ask, I say, "The magistrates want everyone to witness these events, and Ingersoll's is too small. We should leave now."

I gather the afflicted girls so my wife and I can escort them to the meetinghouse.

Two constables follow along—though whether they do so to protect us or hinder us, I'm not sure. I feel stifled and separated from Jehovah. *This is a test,* I tell myself. *Jehovah will see that I am steadfast, and all will be well.*

I lead the witnesses into the meetinghouse through the side door and seat them on the bench directly in front of the magistrates, where they will have a good view of the accused witches, who will be brought to the platform before the bar of justice.

The people crowded into the meetinghouse fall silent as the girls enter. Every possible seat is filled, and more people stand around the sides of the room. I've never seen this venue attended to such an extent. It hurts to believe Jehovah's presence here isn't enough to inspire their attendance on most days, and yet they are enticed here today. What for? Surely not justice. If I'm honest, they seem to only be here for vengeful reasons. They want to watch *punishment.*

Hathorne looks at each witness before raising his hands for silence.

"Let us begin," he says. "Reverend Parris, please offer up a prayer to open the court."

I take my place in front of the bar of justice. Raising my hands and bowing my head, I say the prayer I've been saying since witches began afflicting my family and flock: "Mighty Jehovah, open our eyes to the snares of the enemy, that we may not be deceived by the whispers of evil. Grant the magistrates a discerning spirit to separate truth from falsehood and good from evil, and that we may all walk blamelessly in yer sight. Amen."

Sarah Good

March 1, 1692
Holding Cell, Ingersoll's Ordinary

I can't smoke my pipe without tabak, but I chew the stem and trick my belly so it thinks I've eaten.

Goody Osborne leans against the wall, the elderly woman's face collapsed in exhaustion. The Indian woman still sits in the dark corner. Her breath rasps when she inhales, as if she can't fill her lungs.

I glance at the small window near the rafters. The light is shifting, growing brighter. We have been locked in here for hours.

Finally, the door opens, and four men step inside. One walks up to me.

"Remember me?" Constable Locker asks. "Magistrates are ready for ye now. Stand up. Constable Herrick and I will take ye across."

The men wait until I pull myself to a standing position. Then, each one grabs one of my arms in a grip so tight it feels like their hands claw down to my bones.

I twist and whine. "Too tight, ye be!"

"Don't fight us," Constable Locker growls. "We're taking ye to the meetinghouse so they can decide if ye're a witch."

"Ahm no witch!" I snarl.

The constables pull me forward out of the room and through the ordinary. Behind them, each of the other constables grips a suspected witch. When I step outside, I blink in the bright light. The constables drag me across the pathway and through the side door of the meetinghouse. When we pass the witnesses, all four girls writhe and scream in pain, as if our mere presence is enough to cause them physical harm.

"What's the matter wid dem?" I ask.

"Thought ye might know," Constable Locker says. "Ye're the one that causes them pain."

"Nay, I never hurt dem!"

"Turn the witches so I can see them," a deep voice says.

I face a man sitting behind a long table. His hair hangs to his shoulders, and his doublet is sturdy. His cold eyes peer into me before they move on to the other two women.

"Leave this one," he says pointing at me, "and take the other two back until we're ready for them."

Magistrate John Hathorne

March 1, 1692
Salem Village Meetinghouse

This is the most astonishing scene I've ever witnessed.

Betty Parris, Abigail Williams, Ann Putnam, the Younger, and Elizabeth Hubbard shriek a never-ending cacophony of piercing cries as the constables escort two of the prisoners past them on the way to Ingersoll's Ordinary until it's their turn to be examined by the court. The girls' bodies jerk and twist.

They cry out in response to being pinched and from other tortures no one else can see.

It is most unsettling. I look at the raggedly dressed woman before me, determined she will confess her guilt and expose her evil master. Sarah Good's eyes track everything and everyone in the meetinghouse like a feral forest creature. I've no doubt she serves the devil who now abandons her to face the king's justice alone. I look at the warrant before me. Questioning the witches will not suffice; I want confessions that eliminate the need for a trial. The witches need to be executed before this contagion spreads further.

I nod to the court secretary, Ezekiel Cheever, to begin taking notes. Those in attendance hush, the crowd going silent. Even the girls, despite Sarah's presence, begin to quiet. I glance again at the warrant and begin.

"Ye are Sarah Good," I state in a reasonable voice.

"Aye."

"Tell me," I say gently, "what evil spirit are ye familiar with?"

"None," Sarah rasps.

"Have ye made contact with the devil?"

The woman shakes her head and trembles. "Nay, Yer Worship."

The girls cry out, as if to prove the woman before me lies. I watch them writhe, crying. Tears mask their pale cheeks. Surely, they can't be faking—and yet the woman before me doesn't break eye contact when I speak to her nor does she wince with guilt.

"Do ye hurt these children?" I ask, my voice booming through the room.

She shakes her head, her face flushed. "Nay, I dinna hurt them! I scorn it!"

"Who, then, do ye employ to hurt them?"

Her jaw drops. "I employ nobody."

"What *creature* do ye employ, then?"

She shakes her head again. "No creature. I be falsely accused."

I change tactics, reading through the notes on the case. I see a testimony from Reverend Parris, who supposedly made contact with Sarah. "Ye approached Reverend Parris's home," I say before everybody present. "Ye were begging for assistance."

"Aye," Sarah confirms. I'll test her on trivial things, see if she lies. So far, no lying yet, at least not on matters I can prove to be true. "Me an' me girls needed help. He's a man of God. Thought if anyone migh' help us, it'd be the likes of him."

Fair enough.

I read something else in the notes and say, "Why did ye go away muttering from Reverend Parris's house?"

"I didna mutter. I thanked 'im fer what he gave my child."

"And ye made no contract with the devil?"

"Nay. I swear it," she says in a firm voice.

I turn my attention to the four girls in court—who are now quiet, listening to my questions with undivided attention.

"All of ye, look upon this slatternly woman. Is she the one who hurt ye?"

"Yes," the one called Abigail says. "She was one of them. She's hurt us these past two months, and even this morning."

Elizabeth and Ann echo Abigail's statement while Betty trembles and nods her head.

"I saw her plainly at my house," Ann says. "And also at other times."

"Nay," Sarah murmurs with a panicked expression. "I never touched 'em nor thought evil of them."

The girls start writhing and crying out again.

Ann stares at Sarah. "Stop pinching me!"

"I'm not touching ye! How can I? I'm here and ye across the room!"

"It's *ye*. I saw ye when ye did it," Ann claims again.

"Sarah Good," I intone, "do ye not see what ye have done? Why do ye not tell us the truth? Why do ye torment these poor children?"

Sarah twists her hands together. "Ah dinna torment them!" she exclaims. Then, gesturing to the side door through which the other accused were taken, she says, "Wha' of the others? The women who also stand accused of this? Do ye plan to interrogate them as well, or just pin the blame of this on me?"

I pounce. "Which one of them is guilty? What do ye know?"

Sarah's eyes dart around the room. "'Twas Osborne."

"No," Abigail retorts. "'Twas ye and Goody Osborne *both*."

I breathe deeply, gathering my thoughts for more questions. "Do ye attend meeting on Sunday?"

"Nay," Sarah says. "I would, but I dinna have proper clothes."

"What is it ye say when ye go muttering away from persons' houses?" I ask.

Sarah sighs. "If I must tell, I will tell."

I lean forward in anticipation. "Do tell us, then," I say softly.

"It is the commandments. Ah kin say the commandments, ah hope?" Sarah asks with a cunning smile.

"What commandment is it?"

"If I must tell ye, I will tell. It is a psalm."

"What psalm?"

"The Lord is . . ." Sarah mutters.

"I ask again. Who do ye serve?"

"I serve Jehovah."

"What god do ye serve?"

"The one who made heaven and earth," Sarah answers faintly, her eyes shifting away from me.

Suddenly, a voice from the crowd calls out, "I heard her own husband say he was afraid she was a witch or would soon become one."

"Who speaks?" I demand, eyeing the crowd. Everybody goes silent. No one answers. I realize, in the wake of this statement, that Sarah's husband must be present. "William Good," I say to the crowd of pale faces. "Stand up."

Good cringes and shuffles to his feet. A child clings to his hand.

"Yes, Yer Worship," William responds.

I gesture to the child. "Who stands with you?" I ask.

"My daughter Dorothy," William answers. "Mine and Sarah's."

I make a note. "Did ye ever see Sarah Good do anything suspicious? Anything that revealed an unworldly power?"

"I never saw anything, Yer Worship. But she has a bad carriage. She shuffles and cringes. She steals when she can. She curses people she dislikes. I find myself forced to say with tears in my eyes that she is an enemy to all good."

I pound my gavel. I'm disappointed Sarah Good didn't confess, but there are two other witches to interview.

"I've heard enough to commend Sarah Good for trial. Constable, remove this woman and bring in Sarah Osborne."

Sarah Good

March 1, 1692
Holding Cell, Ingersoll's Ordinary

I chew my pipe. Seems like I been in this room for hours, but perhaps not so long as that.

Wish I had tabak.

The door opens to admit Constable Herrick and Goody Osborne. *She looks like a ghost—or maybe a witch.* I cackle at my private joke.

"Shut yer mouth, witch!" Constable Herrick says. He leans Goody Osborne against the wall and crooks his finger at Tituba, who stands in a dark corner, trying to be invisible. "Ye, there! I'll be back for ye after the magistrates have their dinner. Come quietly, or ye'll wish ye had."

Tituba moans.

"We be hungry," I say.

Herrick walks out and shuts the door.

I chew on my pipe again. The stem's gettin' thin. I have to carve a new one.

Goody Osborne slides down the wall and rests against it with her eyes closed.

"How was it?" I eventually ask.

"He asked me about ye," Goody Osborne says. "Wanted to know if I knew ye. Told me ye said I hurt the children."

"I never did," I lie.

"Asked why I didn't go to meetings. I told him I've been sick for over a year." Goody shakes her head, eyes closed. "Those children . . ."

"Noisy, eh?"

"Said I hurt them, pinched them. I never touched a hair on their heads. I can't even leave my house. Asked me if I saw the devil. How could I?"

"Dey gonna blame us, anyway. May as well tell da truth," Tituba says suddenly from the dark corner of the room.

"The truth?" I ask. Even Goody Osborne's eyes open in surprise. "*Ye talked wid da devil?*"

Tituba's face hardens. "Mebbe."

"Huh." *Maybe there are witches after all. But I'm not one of them.*

I close my eyes. The door opens again.

"Court is back in session," Constable Herrick says. "They want ye now."

I watch Herrick pull Tituba from her corner and take her outside. Master Hathorne is a scary man. Tituba will say whatever he wants to hear.

I have to figure a way out of here. Grab me bairns and run away. But where?

The door opens again, but Herrick doesn't bring in Tituba.

What dey do wid her?

A Constable Braybrook helps Goody Osborne to her feet and leads her out.

"Where's he takin' 'er?" I ask.

"Nervous?" Herrick asks in a gruff voice. "For now, ye come with me. Tomorrow, ye'll go to jail in Ipswich."

"My bairn! My Mercy," I cry.

"She'll come with ye. The other girl, Dorothy, is with her father."

One of the barmaids comes in with my bairn swaddled and wrapped in a shawl. I reach out my arms to fold Mercy in a tight embrace only to panic when the bairn doesn't move. I hold Mercy on my left arm so I can move the shawl back from her face. The babe twitches her lips.

"Did ye feed 'er?"

"Gave her pap when the last prisoner left."

I open my shift. "Got to feed 'er." After a few minutes, Mercy begins to weakly suckle.

"We're leaving now," Herrick says. "She can feed while ye ride pillion."

Herrick keeps his hand around my arm. Three constables join us. Herrick keeps a tight grip, pulling me through the ordinary's main room. Patrons fall silent as we make our way across the space. I keep my eyes on Mercy, who continues to suck weakly at my breast.

Outside, Herrick mounts his horse, and a constable lifts me to the pillion behind his saddle.

I grip the saddle with my free hand, terrified I'll fall off the horse and crack my head open. Eventually, Herrick turns onto the pathway that leads to his farm. An unpainted barn stands near the house. The men dismount and lead their horses inside.

A constable lifts me off the sheriff's mare and takes me into one of the stalls. A brown-and-white cow turns her head from the manger to look at me before returning to her meal. The barn is damp and cold and smells, but there's a roof over our heads, at least.

"Take yer shoes off," Herrick says.

"Why?"

"Remove them, or I'll do it for ye. Take off yer stockings too."

I lower myself to the straw-covered floor to remove my shoes and stockings. My bare feet meet the straw, and I recoil against the chill of it.

A constable comes in with a bowl of porridge. "Dinner," he says.

I take the bowl and tip the contents into my mouth. It tastes heavenly. I think, for some reason, that it would taste better with pork fat—or, better yet, real pork.

"Don't be getting any ideas," Herrick says, stepping away from my stall. I realize he's leaving me here for the night. "Ye'll be off to jail in the morning. And tonight I'm leaving three guards here. I won't like it if they wake me to say ye're gone. Do ye understand me?"

I look at Herrick's stern face and nod.

The guards take straw and make themselves comfortable away from the stalls and in a position blocking the exit. The night grows colder.

I listen closely. The straw begins to rustle as the men settle down for the night. When the sounds of snoring grow steady and deep, I wrap up Mercy and peek around the stall's entry. The men are spread around the doorway, but the door isn't entirely closed. It looks like there is just enough room to slip out. I pause, thoughts racing. I know if I stay here, I'll get the noose.

I've got to try to escape. It's my only chance.

I creep past the guard closest to me. He snorts in his sleep before rolling onto his side.

My heart throbs. The baby shifts. I cover my babe's nose and mouth and creep by the next sleeping guard. The man closest to the door leans against the outside wall, his head collapsed on his shoulder. He sleeps right next to the small, open space. I hold my breath. I step on something sharp with my left bare foot and fight the urge to cry out in pain.

Step-close. Step-close. Step-close.

After the fourth step, I'm outside and exposed under a slightly waning moon. I continue to make careful steps until the house and barn are behind me.

I'm free!

I smile until I remember I have no place to hide.

Elizabeth Hubbard

March 1, 1692
Dr. Samuel Griggs's House

I'm giddy with relief. The court session is over, and I'm back at my chores. I smile as I distribute tankards of small beer to my uncle and his guest, Samuel Sibley.

"It was a grand day," Sibley says. "The magistrates rooted out the forces of evil in our village. They'll not be trying their luck here in the near future."

The men clink tankards.

"Aye," Dr. Griggs replies. "I said there was an evil hand at work afflicting the girls grievously, but I had no idea of its extent."

"Yer girl held up well. Ye're a brave one, Eliza, especially after Tituba admitted to pinching ye this morning."

I flinch. *I won't think of it now.*

Without warning, there's a sharp pain in my belly. I double over and moan. "It hurts!" I roll on the floor and clasp my belly.

"What's happened?" Dr. Griggs asks in surprise.

I turn my head and gasp. My heart pounds, making me dizzy.

"She's here!" I point at the figure. "Master Sibley, Sarah Good stands on the table beside ye. Ye can see her naked breast and bare feet. She's barelegged as well."

I twist in an effort to relieve the intense cramping.

Sibley grabs his walking stick. "Where? Where is she?"

"There, on the table!" I point again at the ghostly figure with the malicious stare and cry against the pain. *She's angry with me for speaking the truth this morning!*

Sibley draws his arms up and swings his stick. *Thwack.* "I can't see anything. Did I hit her?"

The figure skitters before my eyes.

"Yes! Ye hit her across the back. I think maybe ye killed her." *I hope.*

Sibley pants from exertion. "It didn't feel like I hit anything. Where is she now?"

I look at the table, but it's empty. "Gone," I whimper and slump onto the floor.

Dr. Griggs helps me into a chair and hands me his tankard.

"Ye've had a shock, my dear," Dr. Griggs says. "Sit for a moment. Are ye sure she's gone now?"

I peer carefully around the room. "I don't see her . . ."

Dr. Griggs nods at Master Sibley. "Ye either killed the witch or frightened her away, Master Sibley. Well done. Eliza, if ye've recovered sufficiently, bring more beer. We also need to regain our senses."

The room spins when I stand. They continue talking, their attention taken up with the witches rather than the status of my health.

"Master Sibley," my uncle says, "we must report this incident to the magistrates as soon as may be. The girls won't be safe until the witches are executed."

I'm uneasy. *Are there more witches waiting to entrap me? Will any of us ever be safe again?*

CHAPTER

Constable George Herrick

Just after midnight, March 2, 1692
Constable George Herrick's House

Bang-bang-bang!

My wife shakes me awake. "Who's making that infernal racket?"

I roll onto my back, still asleep. "What?"

Bang-bang-bang!

"Can't ye hear it?" my wife exclaims. "Either the witch escaped or killed someone. Go down and see what's going on."

I sigh and get out of bed. It's been a long day, what with those witches. I pull on my breeches and start downstairs. "It's a cold night for this nonsense."

My wife wraps a thick shawl over her shift.

I raise an eyebrow. "Ye're coming down with me?"

"Ye might need backup. Yer assistants are useless. I'm convinced they fell asleep, and she escaped. Or maybe she hit one of them on the head—"

Bang-bang-bang!

"I'm coming!" I shout down the stairs as I descend with my wife behind me. I notice she grabs a thick walking stick near the door.

Bang-bang—

When I swing the door open, Samuel Braybrook nearly falls on top of me.

"What's the meaning this commotion?" I thunder.

"It's the witch, sir," John Willard, one of the two men standing behind Braybrook, says. "She escaped."

"And how did she come to do that?" I demand.

"We don't know," Braybrook says.

I reach for my coat by the door and hand my wife her heavy cloak. I know her well enough to know she's not going to wait in the house until I come back. Besides, she's already putting on her boots.

"Tell me, gentlemen, what task did I set ye?" I inquire bluntly.

"To watch the prisoner . . . but she's not where ye left her."

"Let's look in the barn, shall we?"

I stomp across the yard to the barn with my wife and men trailing after me. It's a clear, bitterly cold night, and I'm angry at the fools who took me away from my nice warm bed. They had but one task, and they couldn't do it. Three large, healthy men—and they couldn't contain one mentally unwell woman, weakened significantly by rough living. *Pathetic.*

Unless it was, indeed, witchcraft she used to escape.

"We were resting here," Braybrook says. "We settled by the door so she couldn't get by us."

"And we mebbe rested our eyes for a few minutes," Willard admits. *I thought as much.*

"But then we realized we couldn't hear her," Braybrook continues, "so we got up to check on her, and she was gone. We looked everywhere, but she isn't here."

My wife wanders over to the cow stall and looks inside. "Master Herrick, ye told me ye removed the prisoner's shoes and stockings to reduce chances of her escape, did ye not?"

I look at my wife and draw my eyebrows together.

"How is that relevant?"

My wife smirks. "Well, there's a woman here without shoes who is nursing an infant. I presume she's yer lost witch."

I look inside the stall. Lo and behold, Sarah Good is there. She detaches her infant from her breast and nestles it in her lap.

"Goody Good, these men told me ye escaped. If so, how came ye to be here?" I ask her.

Sarah chews on her empty pipe. "The men snored, so I let myself out. But I had nowhere to go, so I came back. Can I have tabak for my pipe?"

My wife snorts. "What's that on yer arm? Is it blood?"

Sarah glances at her arm. "I fell," she says. "Scraped da ground."

I turn to my men.

"Braybrook, close the door when my wife and I leave, and stand by it with yer eyes open. Ye two"—I point at my other two assistants—"stand on either side of this cow stall and watch the prisoner. Commit her movements to memory."

"It's too dark to see," Braybrook whines.

"Then find a way to restrain her and listen for any sounds. I am returning to my bed. Do not find any reason to disturb me further. Am I understood?"

"Yes, Constable Herrick," the men mutter and take their assigned places.

Sarah Good

March 2, 1692
On the Road to Ipswich

I sit sideways on a horse's hindquarters with my left hand holding on to Braybrook's saddle and my right holding my baby strapped onto my chest. My feet dangle. Braybrook keeps the horse at a steady walk.

"Ye holding on back there?" Braybrook asks.

"Aye." I mutter and adjust my seat so I don't slip over the horse's side or fall off its back. But would that be such a bad thing? I don't want to go to Ipswich Gaol. Herrick's barn was bad enough. But to actually be locked inside? I'll *never* get free.

"Can't hear ye. Is yer seat secure?"

"Aye!" I shout.

I gaze at the meadows by the roadway. If I could slip off the horse and reach the ground before Braybrook knows what I'm doing, I might be able to cross the meadow and escape into the copse of trees beyond. I slowly inch myself sideways until I barely connect with my seat. I release my left hand, hold both my arms around Mercy, and slip off the back of the horse.

I yelp as I hit the ground—the impact is hard, and my ankles weak—but I find my feet and begin running faster than I've ever run before. The wind combs through my tangled hair and sets fire to the tears burning down my cheeks.

"Hey, come back!" Braybrook shouts from behind.

I don't turn around to look at the horse now barreling across the meadow. I keep myself low to the ground, though it's hard running in a crouch while holding on to Mercy.

Thud! I hear Braybrook hit the ground. His feet pound over the soft soil. I rise out of my crouch and run at a faster gait until my skirts twist around me. Before I can right myself, Braybrook leaps on me and wraps his arms around my body. I cup my arms around my baby and twist to the side with Braybrook on top of me.

"No!" I pant. "Won't go ta jail. Ye and those poxy judges can't make me!"

"Hold still!"

I leave my skirts in Braybrook's hands and twist free of him. I jump up and start running again. Hair flies into my eyes.

"Come back, witch!"

"Ah—" *Pant.* "Ain't—" *Pant.* "No witch!"

I roll my ankle on the uneven ground and pitch forward.

Braybrook grabs my legs and drags me back. Constable and prisoner, we lay entwined on the ground, catching our breath. Braybrook recovers first and crawls up my body until he can secure his arm around my waist and drag me upright.

"Does the bairn breathe?" he asks.

My bairn! I pull the shawl off Mercy's face, which is flushed and red. As if realizing she can, Mercy lets out a weak wail.

"Praise to Jehovah!" Braybrook mutters. "Come on."

Braybrook drags me over to his horse and detaches a length of leather from the saddle.

"Hold on to yer babe," he orders, before throwing me back onto the pillion like a sack of turnips. My back crackles on impact.

"Ye've kilt me!" I gasp.

"I wish 'twere true." Braybrook grimaces and begins looping the leather around my legs, securing them to the pillion. "I've orders to take ye to Ipswich Gaol, and I shall."

I'm entirely secured, with my legs bound tightly together and one arm tied to the saddle. I've lost my chance to escape. There's no way I'll get out of this now.

"Don't make any more trouble," Braybrook orders. I spit into his face. "Try that again, and I'll wrap yer face as well."

"Ye'll nivver put me in jail. Ahm no witch."

He scoffs, unconvinced.

Braybrook swings himself into the saddle and walks the horse back to the road.

The journey continues in silence except for the horse's hooves clopping on the ground's rough surface. I try to reach over my body with my right hand to loosen the ties on my left, but I can't reach that far. And I can't move my legs at all.

My head drops onto my chest. A single, silent tear falls down my face.

I am lost. My soul moans within me.

Ann Putnam, the Younger

March 3,1692
Putnam House

I hum to myself in contentment and play cat's cradle with my sister Deliverance. She's having a difficult time with the string but keeps trying. Behind me, I hear Thomas and Eliza setting dishes on our wooden table for supper. There's a sense of fear in my mind, but I remind myself the witches are in jail and can't hurt me anymore.

Suddenly, a figure flickers next to the fireplace. I turn my head away, refusing to look at it—and yet the heat of its gaze draws me in. Against my will, my eyes fall onto the shape, and I see it's a thin child with large eyes.

"Get away from me!" I mutter, dropping the string. The figure moves forward. Its arms stretch out before it, and ghostly fingers make a pinching motion.

"No!" I leap off my stool, but the figure keeps coming toward me. It wears a loose chemise, and its mouth gapes open as if to swallow me whole. I'm being pinched all over my body. I scream.

Deliverance runs to Papa. My family shrieks in alarm.

"Ann, what's happening?" my father demands.

I shiver and point. "Something is here!"

The figure holds out a book. "Sign it," the ghostly voice says. "And this will stop."

"What do ye see?" Mam asks.

"No, I will never sign yer book!" I say to the figure. To my horror, it moves closer, and I feel it pinch me again. "Ow. Stop it! *Please!*"

I collapse onto the floor and twist to escape the monster.

"Go away!" I cry. "Please, go away!"

I dissolve into sobs of pain and fear.

"*Sign,*" the figure croaks.

"No!"

The figure grabs me, wraps its arms around my neck, and squeezes.

I claw at my throat. I wheeze but can't catch my breath. I fall into darkness.

Samuel Braybrook

March 24, 1692
South of Salem Village

Witches afflict the entire village, and I'm constantly on alert, lest they torment me. I'm the one charged to arrest or transport them, and as such, I'm certain they plan to punish me.

Today I have to arrest a five-year-old child—the daughter of Sarah Good. I suppose witchcraft can be passed on to a child, but the girl has lost so much already. It seems cruel to put her in jail, to accuse her of something so malignant.

I guide my horse to a ramshackle shed south of the village and dismount.

"William Good, ye in there?" I shout.

"Who's askin'?"

"Assistant Constable Braybrook. I'm here to collect yer daughter."

William comes to the doorway, face pale. "What fer?"

"I have a warrant for her arrest."

William's jaw drops. "Why?"

"Suspicion of witchcraft."

"She ain't no witch! She be five," he says, astonished.

His reaction makes me feel unsteady. It's not right, arresting a child. I know that. And yet I've got to follow through on my orders. "I'm no magistrate," I remind him. "I just pick up accused witches and take them to court. Bring her out. If ye resist, then I'll have to arrest ye."

William's face blanches. "Dorothy, girl, come out here now."

An underfed child wearing cast-off clothing that engulfs her small frame emerges at her father's side with wide, fearful eyes.

"Dorothy, ye go with Constable Braybrook," William says. "I'll be along later to fetch ya."

The child doesn't say anything; she just holds out her hands to me.

"Would ye like to ride with me on my horse?" I ask.

Dorothy looks at my horse and then looks at her father, who turns away from her. I'm certain he's sobbing. I put my hands around Dorothy's waist and lift her up to my shoulders, distracting her from her father's tears. I set one of Dorothy's hands on my horse's neck.

"Ye can pet him. He won't hurt ye."

Dorothy strokes my gelding's rough coat, her eyes widening in surprise.

"I'm going to swing ye up into the saddle, and then I'll ride behind ye. And we'll go to the village. Ye'll like it, I promise. Ye can see pretty far from the back of a horse."

After settling Dorothy in front of me, I wrap my arms on either side of her and lift the reins.

"Come to the meetinghouse later," I tell William. "Mebbe ye can take her home with ye."

I turn my horse around and head back to the road. I don't understand how the girl can be a witch. She's too young. But it ain't up to me.

Magistrate John Hathorne

March 24, 1692
Salem Village Meetinghouse

I stretch my shoulders. The afflicted girls and women huddle together in front of the audience of Salem villagers who speak quietly among themselves. The revelation that Rebecca Nurse is a witch shocked them. If a prominent member of the church works for the devil, anyone can.

I shudder at the thought.

"Shall we call it a day, then?" Jonathan Corwin asks me.

"Who else do we have in custody?" I inquire.

"Sarah Good's daughter, Dorothy. Strange to think one so young could be turned. We can wait for another day to examine her."

"Nay. She be here now. Constable Braybrook, bring in the prisoner."

Five minutes later, the one afflicted adult woman and all the girls begin crying out. Braybrook stands in the doorway, holding Dorothy's hand. The child sucks her thumb and is shockingly young.

"Bring her forward," I say.

The constable escorts Dorothy to the platform and steps back. The child looks around the room. She has a fearful demeanor. When her gaze falls on the shrieking witnesses, they begin writhing with pain.

"She's pinching me," one complains.

"Look at my wrist! She bit me!" another asserts and holds out her arm.

"Constable, hold the child's head still so she cannot gaze on those tortured creatures," I suggest, watching Dorothy's face closely.

Braybrook turns the girl's head toward the doorway and holds it there. The child doesn't object. In fact, she makes no sound at all. Curious.

"Free her head," I say.

Dorothy turns slightly, and as her gaze falls on two of the girls, they begin to shriek. I have a sudden urge to block my ears from the incessant noise.

"It has been an exceedingly long morning," I say. "I have heard enough. Master Corwin, I propose to send this child to Salem Gaol with Mistress Nurse. We can interview her at a later time."

Magistrate John Hathorne

March 26, 1692
Jailor William Dounton's House

Dorothy wanders around the garden. She stoops to examine an early spring flower and picks it up. She's an attractive child. A bit undernourished, perhaps, but that's only to be expected in her transient life. Examining a child charged with witchcraft is a new experience. A normal child her age is without guile. But in the case of an accused witch, I don't know what to expect.

"Shall we begin?" Reverend Higginson asks.

"Please proceed, Master Hathorne," Corwin says.

I'm conflicted. All children are born in sin, and the devil can attack children as easily as he does any other honest folk. But the thought that one so young could be tainted bothers me in a way I can't quite articulate. Nevertheless, if witchcraft is afoot, it is my job to ferret it out.

"Come here, Dorothy," I say in a calm voice. I don't wish to frighten the child.

The girl hesitates but comes to me.

"Tell me, Dorothy, do ye have any animals?" I ask. "Any small friend who keeps ye company?"

The child hesitates again. "I have a little snake," she finally says.

"Does it . . . does it take nourishment from ye?" Master Corwin asks.

Dorothy looks puzzled.

"Does it nurse from ye, like a babe from their mother or a calf from a cow?" Reverend Lawson asks.

Dorothy smiles and nods her head. "When it sucks from my hand, it tickles."

We draw in a collective breath of surprise.

"Can ye show us the spot on yer hand where it suckles?" I ask.

Dorothy points to the lowest joint of her right index finger. Carefully, I pick up Dorothy's hand and hold it near my face to examine it.

"Gentlemen," I say. "I see a small, red spot that looks like a flea bite. Do ye concur?"

I pass Dorothy's hand to Corwin, who adjusts his spectacles before peering at the site.

"Yes." Corwin nods. "I see it. It must be a very small snake to have such tiny teeth."

Dorothy pulls back her hand.

"A moment, child," Reverend Lawson says. "I, too, would like to see the mark. May I?"

The child lifts her hand again so Lawson and Reverend Higginson can examine her finger.

"Did someone give ye the snake that sucks yer finger?" Lawson asks.

Dorothy nods her head.

"Who?" I ask.

"My mam."

I jump back from Dorothy, a cold icicle of fear plunging into my heart. This all but confirms our suspicions. *I've heard enough.* "Master Corwin, what more do we need to know? The witch Sarah Good gave her daughter the devil's familiar and brought the child into her nest of witches. Do ye concur, Master Corwin?"

"I do," he says, face grim.

"Jailer Dounton, return Dorothy Good to her cell, where she shall remain with the other accused witches indefinitely."

C H A P T E R

Sarah Good

June 28, 1692
Boston Gaol

Some folks say 'tis summer, but I shiver in the predawn twilight.

Through the small, barred window above our cell, I see a few brave stars twinkling. I wish I could be up there with them instead of in this cell that smells like mold, chamber pots, and vomit. Living rough is better than this. *Cleaner*, even.

Dorothy's soft sobbing pierces the still air, but no one stirs.

"Dinna cry, Dorothy. Mam's here."

The child sniffs and falls silent. *Poor bairn. Couldna save my babe. Can't save ye.*

A shuffle of boots outside breaks the silence. The door swings open to admit several men with lanterns. Constable Herrick stands with gaol keeper John Arnold, flanked by two Salem constables on either side.

"Be sure ye get who we came for," Herrick mutters.

"Susanna Martin, Rebecca Nurse, Sarah Wildes, Elizabeth How, and Sarah Good, stand up," Herrick orders in a loud voice. "We're taking ye to Salem for yer trials today."

171

We moan. Bound by shackles, forced to lean against the damp stone walls—and only days ago, we were all free, living lives normally.

We mourn the life we once had and resent the hopelessness of our life now.

"Quiet," one of the constables orders.

I drag myself upright. "Me girl?" I whisper.

"Not today," the same voice says.

I almost collapse in relief. *Mebbe dey'll forget 'er.*

The constables bind our hands with stout rope before unlocking our shackles and pulling each of us forward into a line. I consider running for the door, but my feet are numb, and just standing makes me feel lightheaded. Besides, I can't leave my girl.

"Dinna fergit me, Dorothy," I whisper. "I weren't a good mam, but I loved ye."

I look into my daughter's blank eyes. *I'm sorry.* A hand grabs my upper arm.

"Come along," Constable Braybrook says gruffly.

The constables tie us onto a wagon. The driver slaps the reins, and we set off.

Possibly for the last time, I watch the golden sun rise from the sea. A tear slides down my face. I pull out my pipe and start chewing the stem.

Sarah Good

June 28, 1692
Court of Oyer and Terminer, Salem Town

Constable Braybrook holds my arm in a tight grip, as if I can escape during the short distance between Salem Gaol and the two-story Salem Town House.

He's right to keep me close after I ran away from him that time. I decide to lean against him.

I drag my feet as much as possible, so he almost has to lift me when he pushes me into a packed room. People stand and sit anywhere they can. The judges sit behind a long table on a raised platform, their collars snowy white against their dark clothing.

I recognize two judges from Salem Village.

On the way to the platform, I pass the same girls who spoke against me before. They start moaning and twisting. Could be they are possessed by the devil—but not by me. I rub the pipe in my pocket.

"Excuse me, Sheriff Corwin," Constable Braybrook says. "After so long in chains, the witch cannot stand on her own."

A youngish man with a harsh face nods and confers with one of the judges. Someone brings out a three-legged stool.

"Much obliged," Constable Braybrook says.

He lowers me onto the stool. "Try not to fall off," he mutters.

A gavel slams loudly against the table.

"*Oyez! Oyez! Oyez!* The court of terminer and oyer is now in session to consider the case of Sarah Good, accused witch."

"Proceed."

A well-dressed, lean young man bows before the judges. "Governor Stoughton, as prosecuting attorney general, I submit the transcripts from Sarah Good's examination by Magistrates John Hathorne and Jonathan Corwin at Salem Village on March 1, 1692, including the testimony of one Tituba who clearly identified Sarah Good as a witch. We also have witnesses to Sarah Good's activities as a witch and to her malicious attacks on her neighbors in Salem. Ann Putnam, please come to the bar."

I stare at Ann Putnam. She walks to the platform with a slight swagger, aware everyone watches her.

I be no witch.

"Tell us about the accused witch, Sarah Good," Judge Hathorne says.

"I first saw Sarah Good on February twenty-fifth of this year," the girl says woodenly. "She pricked and pinched me without mercy, but I didn't know it was her until the next time I saw her two days later, when she tortured me again and urged me to sign her book, but I refused."

Ann looks at me, trembling. The girl looks truly afraid.

"Then," she continues, "during the examination at the meetinghouse in the village, Sarah Good tortured me again. I also saw her afflict little Elizabeth Parris, Abigail Williams, and Elizabeth Hubbard. And I saw her spirit hurt Sarah Bibber."

She shivers and inhales deeply. Those in attendance are silent.

"I believe Sarah Good still bewitches me," Ann declares, raising her chin. I feel the heat of the crowd's attention fall upon me, and I raise my chin in turn. *She lies an' no one stops her! Ahm no witch, and Ahm no' guilty!*

More witnesses come forward to accuse me of harming them.

Susannah Sheldon says that two days ago, I pulled her head behind a chest and tied her hands together and choked her. That William Batten and Thomas Buffington, the Younger had to cut the cords because they were so tight.

I shake my head in denial, but all eyes are on Susannah, who falls into a fit, jerking and crying out in pain. When the fit passes, she says I caused it.

Mary Walcott testifies she saw my image among the witches urging her to write in a book. And then she, too, falls into a fit. When Mary recovers, Susannah says I caused Mary's fit.

"And just now," Susannah says, "I saw invisible hands pick up a saucer from yer table and take it outside. 'Twas Sarah Good who carried it away!"

Sheriff Corwin goes outside and returns with the saucer.

I practically laugh. *How kin it be when I bin sittin' here? It's a trick.*

Sarah Bibber is older than the other witnesses. She's married with a young child. When she passes me to stand before the judges, Goody Bibber shivers. "I saw her torture John Indian and Mercy Lewis, and she beat and pinched me and almost pressed the breath out of my body." Goody Bibber's eyes open widely as she relives her terror. "And then, her figure tortured my child. My precious one cried out and twisted until I couldn't hold on to her. My husband saw what was happening and took the child, but she twisted out of her father's arms. And . . ."

I watch in fascination. Goody Bibber's eyes roll back into her head and her body twists. The woman falls stiffly onto the floor in a fit. Everyone stares at the rigid woman until she revives, their eyes wide and gasps loud.

Goody Bibber points at me. "She stabbed me with a knife!"

"How could I?" I say, desperate for people to see reason. "Ahm sittin' righ' here!"

"It was yer *spirit*. Ye came at me with a knife, and I fell!"

Spectators spring to their feet, surging toward the magistrates. The girls moan and sway. Governor Stoughton bangs his gavel, calling for order. Eventually, the courtroom quiets. A young man stands up.

"Let me see the blade," he demands. "I lost part of my knife here yesterday while the witness was in the room. The blade she holds looks like mine."

Sheriff Corwin holds his hand out to Goody Bibber, who pulls a knife fragment from her skirt. Corwin passes the fragment to the young man who compares it to his own knife. Holding the two pieces together, the man says, "See here! The two pieces fit perfectly. She must have picked up the part I threw away yesterday and held it in readiness."

The room explodes in noise.

Now they know 'tis lies.

"Order. Order!" Governor Stoughton bangs his gavel. "Young man," he says in a loud voice, "ye are dismissed from this court."

"But don't ye want to see the blade?"

"Sheriff Corwin, escort this man outside!"

When the man puts away his knife and leaves, my heart drops. *They will never release me.*

After a short recess, the court calls a witness I remember. I escaped from his barn with my daughter but had no shoes and no place to go. When

Constable Joseph Herrick approaches the witness stand, he does so without looking at me.

"Did the witch stay at yer house?" Magistrate Hathorne asks.

"Aye. Had to transport her from Salem Village to Ipswich, and she stayed in my barn overnight. Put a guard around her, but she escaped. Heard she went to Dr. Griggs's house and afflicted one of the girls. Master Sibley injured her, and she returned. Constable took her to Ipswich the next day."

Ask me, why don' ya? Only got as far as da woods!

I glare at the constable as he lumbers out of the room.

Sarah Gage bustles forward to the witness position before the judges and swears she will tell the truth.

"That woman," Goody Gage says, pointing at me, "came to my house for shelter. As if I'd allow anyone who slept rough to enter my home, especially with smallpox about. I turned her away from my door. Then, she wanted me to give her something to eat, but I told her to be gone. That's when she got to muttering. The next day, one of our cows died. A healthy cow, it was. Dead all of a sudden. For no reason. 'Twas witchcraft!"

No more than ye deserved. But it wasn't by my hand.

Sarah Good

June 29, 1692
Court of Oyer and Terminer, Salem Town

"Mistress Abbey, are ye familiar with the accused witch, Sarah Good?"

"I am," the woman replies. I glare at her. "It were three years ago. She and her husband and child came to us. They had nothing, and out of charity we allowed them to live on our property. But they had no gratitude."

She looked down her nose at me. And 'er husband too.

"How so?"

"She were spiteful and malicious to me, my husband, and our children, until we could no longer have them in our house. We sent them away, for quietness's sake, but she continued to be spiteful, and we began to lose cattle. Perfectly healthy cows began dropping. We lost seventeen head within two years, and also sheep and hogs. She practiced witchcraft on them. And the day she was arrested, we had a cow that could not rise, but as soon as she was arrested, the cow was well."

"This court has heard enough," Governor Stoughton says. "Rise, Sarah Good."

Sheriff Corwin grabs my arm and turns me to face the twelve presiding magistrates. *They all look so sure of themselves. So certain they know the truth. But they be wrong. Ahm no witch!*

"After listening to yesterday's testimony, the court requested Master Newton to draw up three indictments. Sarah Good, ye are indicted for afflicting and torturing Goody Bibber. Ye are indicted for afflicting and tormenting Elizabeth Hubbard. Ye are further indicted for afflicting, torturing, and bewitching Ann Putnam, the Younger. Do ye confess to these crimes?"

"Nay!" I shake my head and stamp my foot. "Never did anythin'. Ahm no' a witch."

"The evidence proves that ye are. I urge ye to confess yer crimes before yer execution, so it may be well with yer soul," Governor Stoughton says before banging his gavel.

"Sheriff Corwin, return the witch to the gaol and bring in Susanna Martin."

How can they believe all those lies? How can they think I can be in two places at once? That I'm strong enough to inflict such harm?

Corwin hands me off to a constable I don't know, and I let him drag me out. The cell's comfortable darkness seems safe. Mayhap I'll die here.

Sarah Good

July 19, 1692
Salem Gaol

I scrape out the last lumps of gruel with my fingers. No one else is eating. I could ask for their portion but don't.

Goody Dounton, the old woman who brings us gruel twice daily, collects the bowls.

"Won't be long now," she says. "Looks like most of ye didn't have much of an appetite." She cackles as she leaves the cell. The screeching of it rubs my raw nerves like a dull nutmeg grater, and I have to clench my fingers into fists to resist screeching back.

My Dorothy . . . Where is she? Will she remember me?

I don't have much time to think on it, for Sheriff Corwin and four constables arrive. Each holds a length of stout rope. A young constable approaches me where I sit, chained to the wall. He pulls me up and twists my body so he can tie my hands behind my back. The thick hemp rope bites into my wrist. After he secures my hands, the man unlocks the shackles binding my ankles and pushes me into the line of five women being prodded outside.

The summer air is sweet and the sunlight beautiful, and I feel myself break over never again seeing another summer in my life. Again, my heart begs for my child.

Without the use of our hands, we all awkwardly mount an old wooden wagon harnessed to a single horse. The driver keeps his back to us. Someone ties me to the wagon's side.

"Begin," Sheriff Corwin orders, and the cavalcade of wagon and constables slowly moves away from the gaol onto Prison Lane to make its way up Essex Street. Along the side of the road, people watch us in silence. The wagon lurches onto Bridge Street and traverses the town bridge over North River.

I turn my head and look up to see Gallows Hill looming ahead. My chest fills with dread.

The barren cliff face slopes down to a ledge at its base. The wagon halts. Constables release the ropes. Someone grabs my arm and pulls me out of the wagon. A copse of sturdy trees stands nearby. A constable I don't know pushes me toward a tree with a ladder in front of it and forces me to climb up several steps. There's a noose dangling from a tree branch.

Always thought I'd starve to death. Didna think I'd hang.

The constable ties my skirts and legs tightly.

I look at the growing crowd that came to gawk and spit in their direction.

A clergyman steps forward, faces the crowd, and excoriates them for disobeying Jehovah. If witches wandered among them, it was because they had failed in their duty to Jehovah. They were not without culpability here, and he made that clear. The crowd appears chastened by his words, and I've a feeling that the meetinghouse will be fuller than ever before now.

After a final prayer, the cleric turns toward our line of convicted witches.

When he stops in front of me, I realize he's a cleric from the Salem Town church. He was at my examination and later at my trial. *Hypocrite!*

"Sarah Good, hear me," he calls, "I am Reverend Noyes, here to release yer immortal soul to Jehovah. Do ye confess to the sins of consorting with the devil and harming Ann Putnam, Goody Bibber, and Elizabeth Hubbard?"

"Nay!" I bellow with all my strength.

"Come now," he says softly, "admit yer guilt. The court proved ye a witch. Confess for the sake of yer soul and the peace of this community."

"Ye lie!" I spit out the words. "I'm no more a witch than yer a wizard, and if ye take away my life, Jehovah will give ye blood to drink!"

The man steps back in horror. Someone ties a burlap hood over my head. The material is coarse and heavy, blocking out everything except for a few pinpricks of light between the thick fibers. The ladder falls away beneath my feet. The rope behind my neck tightens. I want to rip it away, but my hands are tied.

Crack!

I try to gasp but can't. The words "receive me" flash across my mind. My thoughts fall into darkness. From another dimension, I watch my body convulse and sway at the end of the rope. Back and forth. Back and forth. Until all becomes still, and I am free.

AUTHOR'S NOTE

The Life & Times of Sarah Good, Accused Witch is the prequel to the Salem Stories series. None of the characters have a direct connection to the Derby or Crowninshield families. However, no one in Salem escaped the trauma caused by the witchcraft hysteria of 1692. *The Life & Times of Sarah Good* is a work of historical fiction inspired by seventeenth-century Salem. The names of individuals refer to real persons, and the story is based on primary research materials.

In 1672, Salem Village, with a population of about three hundred fifty people, separated from Salem Town. Villagers were granted authority to hire a minister, build a meetinghouse, and collect taxes.

The village had a fractious relationship with its ministers. The first minister the village called, Reverend James Bayley, served from 1672–1679. He was followed by Reverend George Burroughs (1680–1683) and Reverend Deodat Lawson (1684–1688) before Reverend Samuel Parris accepted the pulpit in 1689.

Salem villagers did not provide a large compensation package. The villagers paid Reverend Bayley forty pounds annually. In 2017, this was the equivalent of £4551, enough money to purchase six horses.

In 1689, Reverend Parris received an annual salary of sixty-six pounds, plus firewood. The firewood often was not forthcoming. Ministers did not receive their entire salary in cash. The majority of compensation came in the form of country cash. This could be a calf's head, a swarm of bees, milk, cheese, and so forth.

The Salem Witch Trials officially began on March 2, 1692 with the examination of Sarah Good, Sarah Osborne, and Tituba, who were all accused of afflicting Abigail Williams, Betty Parris, Ann Putnam, and Elizabeth Hubbard. The three accused witches were bound over for trials.

Bridget Bishop was hanged on June 10, 1692, the first witch to be convicted and executed for witchcraft.

From June 30 and into early July 1692, the court of oyer and terminer convicted Sarah Good, Elizabeth Howe, Susanna Martin, Sarah Wildes, and Rebecca Nurse of witchcraft. All were executed by hanging on July 19, 1692.

By the time the trials ended in 1693, over two hundred people had been arrested for witchcraft. Nineteen people were hanged, and one person was pressed to death for refusing to enter a plea.

Dorothy Good

Dorothy Good remained in Boston Gaol until December 10, 1692, when Samuel Rea of Salem paid a bond of fifty pounds to release her from prison. Dorothy had been incarcerated, often in chains, since the previous March and was no longer in her right mind. It appears Dorothy then went to live with her father, who had married Elizabeth Drinker in 1693. From time to time, William Good received charity from Salem selectmen.

In May 1710, the colonial legislature appointed a committee to hear petitions for restitution from families who suffered financial loss from the witch trials. William Good petitioned the committee for funds to support his daughter Dorothy who was then twenty-two years old. Good reminded the committee that Dorothy's mother had been executed, that her infant sister had died in jail, and that Dorothy herself had been chained in a dungeon. Since that time, Dorothy had been chargeable and unable to govern herself. The term *chargeable* referred to the financial burden of her care. The committee awarded William Good thirty pounds sterling, one of the largest sums granted. There is some evidence that Dorothy did not always reside with her father. Between 1708 and 1715, Dorothy resided in Benjamin Putnam's household at William Good's expense. In 1711, William Good died.

Dorothy reappeared in Salem records in September 1720 when town selectmen *warned* Dorothy out of town. Transient persons, particularly unwed mothers, were warned out of towns so the town would not be responsible for financial support of the unwed mother or her child.

In November 1720, Salem paid Nathaniel Putnam for keeping Dorothy Good and her infant for eleven weeks. It appears Dorothy remained with the Putnams for several years. In 1722, Dorothy's daughter Dorothy was indentured to Nathanial Putnam to be trained as a house servant until she reached the age of eighteen or married. During this time, she would work as a servant in exchange for housing, food, clothing, and basic literacy.

Dorothy then moved to the household of Robert Hutchinson, Nathaniel Putnam's brother-in-law. Later that same year, Dorothy was sent to the house of corrections where Salem sent able-bodied people who loitered, wandered from place to place, or lived disorderly lives in general. Dorothy remained in the house of corrections for eighteen weeks and then returned to Robert Hutchinson's household.

Three years later, records indicate Dorothy was again in the house of corrections and apparently pregnant. In June 1725, Dorothy was in Concord when she gave birth to a son she named William. Concord selectmen paid a Nathaniel Billing for taking care of Dorothy Good during her lying-in at his house. In October, Dorothy was back in Salem, living in Robert Hutchinson's household. She eventually resided in Jonathan Batchelder's household for ten years. Batchelder died in 1738, and Dorothy Good disappeared from the public record until 1761.

On August 14, 1761, the *New London Summary* reported that a deceased woman identified as Dorothy Good was found in a bog near New London. Whether the name referred to Dorothy Good the elder, or the younger, is unclear.

Reverend Samuel Parris

On November 18, 1694, in an effort to calm ongoing strife in Salem Village, Reverend Parris read out a statement he called "Meditations for Peace." Parris admitted that witchcraft broke out in his house, saying someone had used diabolical means to raise spirits, by which he meant fortune-telling and efforts at counter magic, such as the witch cake. Parris stated he was wrong to accept the reports of those possessed because he now realized evil could impersonate the innocent.

Parris insisted he was careful in taking notes from the examinations in court. He admitted that when he spoke as a witness under oath, he referred to apparitions, not physical bodies. Parris apologized for unwise statements he made in his sermons and said he now sympathized with those who had been accused of witchcraft and their families.

On November 26, 1694, Parris read out the charges church dissenters made against him, again read his "Meditations for Peace," and said that in 1692 he had done what he thought was his duty, but that he might have been mistaken.

On June 21, 1696, Parris formally announced that he would step down as minister at the end of July, which he did. However, he refused to vacate the parsonage until he received payment for his services. The Essex County Court verified that Parris's salary was sixty-six pounds annually, and that it had not been fully collected from 1691–1695. The court ordered the village rates committee to collect the funds and pay Parris before court convened in September 1691. The next court convened but no mention was made of the matter. Parris remained at the parsonage.

In March 1697, Salem Village sued Parris to remove him from the parsonage. Parris countersued for his unpaid salary and noted that if he left the parsonage, he would never receive the funds. The court ruled in favor of Parris and ordered the village to pay court costs. The Village appealed. The matter went to arbitration, and on August 30, 1697, the arbiters ordered Parris to relinquish his deed to the parsonage and its lands. The arbiters also ordered the village to pay Parris seventy-nine pounds, nine shillings, and six pence.

The village paid Parris the sum ordered by the court. On September 24, 1697, Parris wrote a quit claim for the parsonage and moved away.

Reverend Joseph Green

In November 1697, Salem Village invited Reverend Joseph Green to preach. In December, they offered him the pulpit with a salary of sixty pounds the first year and seventy pounds the next. Green accepted, but conscious of previous fractious relations between Salem Village and their minister, he stipulated that if they began to quarrel, he would consider himself released from the arrangement. The same ministers who ordained Reverend Samuel Parris ordained Joseph Green in November 1698.

Ann Putnam, the Younger

Ann's mother Ann Putnam, the Elder died of unknown causes on May 24, 1699, and her father Thomas Putnam, the Younger on June 8, 1699. The almost simultaneous deaths left Ann Putnam, the Younger to look after her younger siblings ranging in age from one to eighteen.

In 1706, at the age of twenty-nine, Ann asked to join the church at Salem Village. Reverend Green interviewed Ann and composed an account of her conversion experience and her confession about her involvement in the witch trials of 1692.

While Ann stood silently before the congregation, Reverend Green read her confession in which she admitted that while she was a child she had accused "several persons of a grievous crime, whereby their lives were taken away from them, whom now I have just grounds and good reason to believe they were innocent persons." Ann begged "forgiveness from God and from all those unto whom I have given just cause of sorrow and offense."

The Salem Village church admitted Ann Putnam, the Younger into full communion. Ann died in 1715.

Digitized copies of original source materials relating to the Salem Witch Trials are available at the *Salem Witch Trials Documentary Archive & Transcription Project* compiled by the University of Virginia. These can be accessed at https://salem.lib.virginia.edu/home.html

The Salem Witch Trials: A Day-by-Day Chronicle of a Community Under Siege by Marilynne K. Roach offers a daily account of events surrounding the trials.

The Life & Times of Sarah Good, Accused Witch is a work of historical fiction inspired by the Salem Witch Trials of 1692. It is not a work of biography or nonfiction.

PREVIEW FROM AMBITION, ARROGANCE & PRIDE: FAMILIES & RIVALS IN 18TH CENTURY SALEM

(SALEM STORIES BOOK 1)

Chapter 1

Mary Hodges

1735

The smattering of raindrops on the windowpanes that February afternoon matched Mary's mood. She sat before her mother, facing an oval mirror propped upon a small mahogany dressing table as she twisted her hair into braids. The candles on either side of the mirror flickered in the draft.

"You'll have to make a braid and pin it under your cap." Mary's mother—who was known to everybody else strictly as Mrs. Hodges—pulled Mary's hair straight back. "Perhaps like this?"

"Don't pull so hard. You're hurting me."

Mrs. Hodges ignored her daughter, made a tight braid, and secured it with several long silver hairpins.

"Even out your face powder," Mrs. Hodges directed.

Mary covered her eyes with a handheld mask and brushed a rice powder concoction over her entire face.

Mrs. Hodges turned her daughter's chin. "Now your face is too pale. Add a bit of rouge."

Mary rolled her eyes. "Rouge makes me look like an overripe apple. I look better without anything on my face."

"And show your freckles?" Mrs. Hodges gasped. "Not on your marriage day. Add more rouge to your lips. And put this patch on. You can wear it on your right cheek today."

Mary opened a small container and flicked through several black fabric stars, half-moons, and dots before selecting a small star and placing it on her right chin line near her lips. Mary tilted her head. "What do you think, Mother?"

Mrs. Hodges squeezed her daughter's shoulders and looked at her face in the mirror. "I think you look bonny."

Mary reached up to touch her mother's hand.

"Is it a bad omen to have such cold weather on my marriage day?"

Mrs. Hodges eyed her daughter's expanded belly. "I think, in this instance, it would be a worse omen to delay. Now, stand up so I can finish dressing you. Put your shoes on first."

Mary put on a pair of small white leather pumps, each with a low heel, and stood before her mother, who added panzers to plump out Mary's hips.

Mary laughed. "I don't think I need extra padding."

"It will balance your belly. Stand up straight and spread your arms out."

Mrs. Hodges added an embroidered petticoat, securely cinching its ribbons, before placing a matching stomacher over the loose corset.

"Now slip your arms into the dress."

The peach silk garment floated over Mary's petticoat, its three-quarter sleeves tipped in lace. Mrs. Hodges's eyes teared.

"Beautiful," she whispered. "And now, the mantua."

Mrs. Hodges placed the white lace cap with its sheer, flowing train over Mary's bundled hair.

"Are you ready?"

Mary's eyes sparkled to match her smile. "Never more so."

Ambition, Arrogance & Pride is available in ePub, Print, and Audio editions at Amazon.

GLOSSARY OF TERMS & NAMES

Battle at Bloody Brook—September 28, 1675. Warriors from the Pocumtuc Confederacy and their allies destroyed a company of militia escorting a convoy of wagons carrying the harvest from Pocumtuc to Hadley in the Connecticut River Valley.

Braybrook, Samuel—Assistant/deputy constable, Salem Village.

cat's cradle—A string game played with two or more people who make shapes out of string in various formations.

caudle—A hot drink of thin gruel mixed with wine or ale and sweetened or spiced. It was prepared over the fire in the birthing chamber and taken by the mother and her attendants during the delivery, thus nourishing the mother and providing a tipple for those with her.

clout—From Old English for cloth. Small squares of cloth that might be used with babies under swaddling, or for catching menstrual flow, or anything that only requires a small bit of cloth such as a doll's dress.

coif—White linen cap Puritan women wore over their hair buns.

coinage—In 1652, the Massachusetts Bay Colony struck a series of silver coins. The date was used on all subsequent coins because it was after Charles I's execution, so the colony was not in violation of prohibition against colonial coining.

- Pine Tree Shilling – On the coins, the lettering *MASATHUSETS IN* circles a pine tree. Reverse has inscription *NEW ENGLAND AN DOM 1652* and Roman numeral *XII* (for 12 pence = 1 shilling).

- Oak Tree Coins—Silver coins minted in Massachusetts, 1652–1667. Feature oak tree with shrub on either side and two base lines below. Oak is symbol of wisdom, strength, endurance, and longevity. Coins struck by Hull & Sanderson in Boston. This is a 2-pence coin. It's the only coin with a date different from 1652. Denominations of 6 pence, 3 pence, 2 pence.
- Willow tree icon worth a shilling minted in Boston under direction of mint master John Hull and his assistant Robert Sanderson.

Flint, Captain Thomas (1645–1721)—Salem Village. Carpenter. Selected to build the first meetinghouse. Owned over 900 acres of land. Wounded at the Great Swamp Fight. Involved in efforts to establish a church for Salem Village.

Great Swamp Fight—December 19, 1675. Key battle during King Philip's War fought between the New England colonial militia and the Narragansett people.

Herrick, Corporal Joseph (1645–1717)—Constable of Salem during witch trials. Fought in King Philip's War when he was age forty-seven.

Honorific Titles:

- Master/Mister. Gentlemen, professional men, substantial citizen, literate tradesman, skilled artisan, successful merchant, large landowner.
- Mistress. Wife of a master.
- Goodman. Middle-class man who was settled, staid, married, and of lower social rank than a master.
- Goodwife/Goody. Wife of a goodman.

Ingersoll, Nathaniel (1632–1718)—Salem Village. Owned Ingersoll's Ordinary. Member of militia, first as corporal, then sergeant, then lieutenant. Church deacon.

King Philip's War, aka First Indian War (June 20 1675–1676)—Named after
Wampanoag sachem Metacom, also known as King Philip. Hostilities
initiated by colonists at Plimoth who hanged three Wampanoag warriors for murdering a praying town native who served the colony as an
informant. Young warriors retaliated by attacking isolated homesteads.
Conflict spread throughout Massachusetts in the summer and fall of
1675. In August 1676, Metacom died in battle. Pequot and Mohegan
people allied with colonists. The Treaty of Casco Bay, formally ending
the war, signed April 12, 1676.

Lathrop, Captain Thomas (1613–1675)—Commanded troops raised in Essex
County to fight in King Philip's War. He was killed at Battle of Bloody
Brook, September 28, 1675.

Metacom aka King Philip—Killed about August 12, 1686.

King William's War (1688–1697)—Also known as the Second Indian
War. Conflict between England and France in North America, with
the English allied with the Iroquois Confederacy and the French allied with the Wabanaki Confederacy. In January 1692, Wabanaki Chief
Madockawando and Father Louis-Pierre Thury led two to three hundred Wabanaki in a surprise attack on York, Maine. The English believed the indigenous people received aid from the French or Dutch. The
French thought the indigenous people were working with the English.
Essentially a conflict between the English and the Iroquois Confederacy
vs. France and the Wabanaki Confederacy.

Narragansett People—During King Philip's War, colonists believed the
Narragansetts harbored Wampanoag refugees at their palisade fortress
where the Great Swamp Fight occurred.

nooning—Term for a rest or meal at midday.

ordinary—An eating house or tavern where public meals were provided at
a fixed price.

pap—Made from cereal mixed with milk as food for babies.

pillion—A cushion placed behind the main saddle of a horse so a second person can ride on horseback.

Plimoth—Seventeenth century spelling for Plymouth.

Sassamon, also called John Sassamon (ca. 1620–1675)—A "praying Indian" who was assassinated in January 1675. Three Wampanoag men were convicted of his murder and executed. These events led to King Philip's War.

small beer—A mildly alcoholic drink consumed from the Middle Ages through the nineteenth century at a time when drinking water was not safe and milk was too expensive for most people. Small beer has an alcoholic volume (ABV) of 2.8%.

venus glass, or fortune-telling with an egg—Folk superstition for predicting who a person might marry. The process: Separate an egg. Slip the white into a glass of water. It will form shapes as it floats. Practitioners examined the shapes to predict the questioner's future husband. For example, if the white looked like a ship, he would be a sailor. If the shape was a plow, he would be a farmer.

Wampanoags—Native American people in the Northeastern Woodlands who lived in southeastern Massachusetts and parts of eastern Rhode Island.

Willard, John—Assistant/deputy constable in Salem Village, 1692.

winding sheet—Fabric covering for a corpse. In the early seventeenth century, faces were not concealed. Men would be dressed in cap and shirt, then wrapped in a linen winding sheet; females were dressed in a shift with a ruffle-edged cap and winding sheet. Face was fully visible. The large piece of fabric was gathered at both ends and could be gathered over the head with an opening for the face.

witch cake—An antidote to witchcraft. Ingredients included rye meal mixed with a small amount of the afflicted's urine. The cake was then baked and fed to a dog which might be the witch's familiar. It was thought the essence of the witch would be in the afflicted person's urine and thus, when the dog ate it, it would injure the responsible witch who might reveal herself.

witch's mark—A mark on the body indicating an individual was a witch. Believed to be a permanent marking made by the devil when the witch was initiated into service with him.

ABOUT THE AUTHOR

Sandra Wagner-Wright holds a doctoral degree in history and taught American and women's history at the University of Hawai'i for over twenty years. She lives in Hilo, Hawai'i. *The Life & Times of Sarah Good* is Sandra's sixth work of historical fiction. Connect with Sandra on social media and at www.sandrawagnerwright.com. Subscribe to her newsletter for updates on blog posts and future projects.

CONNECT WITH SANDRA:

Facebook: https://www.facebook.com/SandraWagner-Wright

LinkedIn: https://www.linkedin.com/in/sandrawwright/

Bluesky: https://bsky.app/profile/sandraww.bsky.social

X (formerly Twitter): https://twitter.com/SandraWWright

QUESTIONS & TOPICS
FOR DISCUSSION

1. What is your first impression of Sarah Solart? Describe her personality.

2. Describe the Putnam family dynamics.

3. What is your first impression of Salem Village? Does the village change much between 1672 and 1692?

4. Do you think the selection process appointing Reverend Bayley minister for the Salem Village church was fair?

5. What was your first impression of Reverend James Bayley?

6. Describe the relationship between Ann Carr and her sister Mary Carr Bayley. Do you think Ann is too dependent on Mary?

7. In the story, Thomas Putnam's attraction to Ann Carr starts the moment they meet. What do you think of their courtship?

8. How is Thomas Putnam affected by the battle at the swamp in North Kingston, Rhode Island?

9. As the years go by, Thomas Putnam's expectations are disappointed. First by the bloody swamp battle, then his wife's inheritance falling through. Finally, and most bitterly, Thomas's father bequeaths the bulk of his estate not to Thomas, his eldest son, but to Joseph, the youngest. And then there are Thomas's nightmares. What kind of man has Thomas become by 1692?

10. How does Sarah Solart fare after her father's death? What is her situation when she agrees to marry Daniel Poole?

11. Did Daniel Poole marry Sarah because he thought she would inherit from her father's estate? Did he care for her?

12. How does Daniel Poole's death affect Sarah emotionally and economically? What becomes of her?

13. Why does William Good marry Sarah? Do you think their marriage was a happy one?

14. How does Sarah fall into poverty?

15. What do you think of Reverend Samuel Parris? How well does he get along with the other villagers? What type of sermons does he preach?

16. Why do you think the witchcraft hysteria engulfed Salem Village?

17. Why do you think Thomas Putnam became so committed to ferreting out witches? Was he afraid of witchcraft? Trying to protect his daughter? Trying to protect his reputation as a village leader? What do you think?

18. Why did people think Sarah Good was a witch?

19. Were the women and girls who accused Sarah Good honest in their charges? Did they experience the physical pains of pinching or were they caught up in their own fear?

20. What do you think of Magistrate John Hathorne? Was he looking for the truth or did he just want a quick conviction of Sarah Good and other accused witches?

21. Do some villagers—for example, Samuel Braybrook—begin to have second thoughts about the alleged witches? Do their doubts make any difference?

22. Was Sarah Good's trial fair? Once accused of witchcraft, was there any chance Sarah would be declared innocent?

OTHER BOOKS BY SANDRA WAGNER-WRIGHT

Fiction

Salem Stories Series

Ambition, Arrogance & Pride: Families & Rivals
in 18th Century Salem (Book 1)
Sea Tigers & Merchants: A New American Generation (Book 2)

Women of Determination & Courage Series

Saxon Heroines: A Northumbrian Novel
Two Coins: A Biographical Novel
Rama's Labyrinth: A Biographical Novel

Nonfiction

Ships, Furs, and Sandalwood: A Yankee Trader in
Hawai`i 1823–1825 (edited journal)

History of the Macadamia Nut Industry in Hawai`i:
From Bush Nut to Gourmet's Delight

The Structure of the Missionary Call to the Sandwich
Islands 1796–1830: Sojourners Among Strangers